DEATH ZONE

The metal-armored men of C.A.D.S. were nearly at the White Sands base and should have heard the identity-challenge code on their channel 32. But the airwaves were silent. As they passed between two sandstone pillars the howl of the desert wind became a mournful sound, a sound that seemed to say: "There is nothing ahead but death."

"Form up!" Colonel Dean Sturgis ordered. "We're going in on full alert, sealed and ready for battle!"

They stormed over the hill like gleaming black titans from another planet, super-running toward their home base, their steel cleats making deep gouges in the hard-packed soil. Heading toward the only place on earth any one of them could call home.

They stormed over the hill — and found only devastation. . . .

CADS

#8 CYBERTECH KILLING ZONE

JOHN SIEVERT

ZEBRA BOOKS
KENSINGTON PUBLISHING CORP.

ZEBRA BOOKS

are published by

Kensington Publishing Corp.
475 Park Avenue South
New York, NY 10016

First printing: November, 1989

Printed in the United States of America

Chapter One

The thin blond man waited anxiously for the scudding clouds to obscure the half-moon hanging over the Soviet-occupied town of Hartsdale, South Carolina. Finally it happened, and the rolling lawn around the broadcast tower was plunged into near-darkness. Relieved, he said a brief prayer for luck, then quickly glanced at his Rolex's luminous dial. Exactly 12:10 A.M. Time to escape.

The man took a deep breath — he was afraid of heights and it took great courage to put first one leg, then the next, over the balcony rail. His slippery patent-leather shoes were not made for climbing, so the escapee had to grope around for a sickening second before his soles made purchase on the first of the many knots tied in the rope.

Hand over hand, grunting in effort, he slowly moved down. It was a descent of just seventy feet. Not much for an athletic type, but he was hardly that. He was Jerry Jeff Jeeters, TV minister of the "new" Gospel. He was the frothing-at-the-mouth, Bible-pounding minister of the new religion that told Americans that it was God's will that they obey their Soviet overlords. But Jeeters was also a spy — a spy for the old, true America that he railed against on the airwaves; a spy for the

America which he cursed on the airwaves night after night.

And now it was time to show his true colors—red, white and blue. Jeeters, on this warm summer night—though his masters didn't know it yet—had just finished his last broadcast for them. He knew that his cover was about to be blown, so he had to dare this escape.

In the pocket of Jeeters's powder-blue suit was a secret report, a report that a man had died for to deliver into Jeeters's hands. A report that had to reach the Revengers, the local anti-communist guerrilla force. Or else the last hope of freedom would die.

Seconds seemed like hours as Jeeters slowly, carefully descended. When he hit ground, Jeeters heard the whistle signal—sort of like a catbird practicing its dawn song. Only it wasn't a catbird, it was Rufus McMaster, his contact man. He *hoped*.

Jerry whistled back twice, a poor imitation of the bird, but it was the reply to tell McMaster that it was really him.

The reverend stepped into the shrubbery, breathing heavily. Then he was bear-hugged. "We have only five minutes to get to the perimeter fence before the patrol comes back," McMaster said. In the dark Jeeters made out a burly khaki-clad bearded man. A man who needed a bath badly—from his smell.

"Okay," Jeeters gasped. "Let's go."

"Wait a second." McMaster jerked violently on the rope, but it didn't come loose. He looked up in consternation and whipped it again, then turned to the minister and whispered, "Didn't you put a slip-knot on it?"

"What's a slip-knot?"

"Well, that's just fine!" McMaster said in exasperation. "They'll spot that rope any minute now—come on!"

Jeeters nodded, and he and the Revenger ducked

6

into the first clump of bushes.

The searchlight that was mounted on the huge spindle top of the WSOV broadcast tower that had been Jerry's home and prison for six years suddenly came on. It swung to the very spot where they had just been standing, and moved on. Evidently the inattentive soldier manning the spotlight hadn't noticed the dangling rope. Luck. But luck favors the *swift!*

They ran across fifty feet of open ground to the next safety stop — some high weeds in a wet area.

The spotlight passed by again, panning across the grass toward the fence of electric charged wire. "You okay?" McMaster asked. "If not, I can carry you."

Jerry looked hard at the big man and decided that McMaster probably could carry him. "No, I can manage. I don't get weak-kneed, I just get out of breath. I'm okay."

They zigged and zagged along a route McMaster checked out with a mini-mine detector, and were within twenty feet of the fence. Then they had company. McMaster pushed Jeeters down into some tall reeds and dropped down beside him.

Now Jeeters too saw the patrol. McMaster cursed under his breath. Just two men — but they shouldn't be there! The Reds must have altered their patrol schedule again!

The Revenger saw the two men sit down and turn their flashlights off. One Soviet lit a match, held it to a plastic cylinder. What the hell was going on? Soon McMaster smelled a strong gym sock-like odor —

Crack! They're smoking crack, he realized.

"Jeeters," McMaster whispered, "you've got to help on this. We can get behind them, where they are sitting down — next to that clump of birch. While I kill the big one," McMaster took out his large knife, "you cover the left one's mouth. Keep him from shouting out. I'll do the rest."

"I — I've never done any killing."

"Yeah, I know. Just hold the little guy's mouth."

They crept up as silently as possible. The search-beam crossed the two soldiers, who just waved. Evidently their buddy was up in the tower, aware they were out there smoking. The spotlight didn't pause a second before passing onward. The pair of Americans were soon in position. And Jeeters's heart pounded like a tom-tom.

"Now," McMaster whispered. Jeeters lunged from the copse of trees and grabbed the small one's mouth. He felt hot crack-breath exhaled between his fingers, and the man emitted a muffled cry. Jeeters heard a short sharp intake of air to his right. Then McMaster was in front of Jeeters's man, jamming his bowie knife upward under the Soviet's rib cage. His man's neck jerked, and the Red stopped trying to bite Jeeters's fingers, then slumped.

"You can stop holding the guy's mouth now."

Jeeters let go. His whole body felt clammy and there was gurgled blood on his hands.

"You okay?" McMaster asked, looking worried.

"Yeah," Jeeters said, "I'm okay, praise the Lord."

Another hundred yards of ducking between bushes and reeds and they were at the fence. In the dim light of the moon penetrating wispy clouds, Jeeters noticed that there were two bulges about five feet apart on the three-wire fence. "Those bumps are Revenger short-circuit devices," McMaster said. "It cuts off the electricity by grounding it with a piece of wire. "After you," McMaster said, standing and pulling the two upper strands of barbed wire apart for Jerry to step through.

The minister caught a pocket and tore it. "Damn," he said. He started to apologize for the blasphemy, and then he almost laughed. He didn't have to be the TV holy man anymore! It didn't matter either, now, that his polyester suit was torn. Smiling, the minister stepped through the fence out into free America—the free America that only existed now in the night!

Once they had reached the huge misshapen oak trees that marked the beginning of the mutant woods, there were more men, and horses. There were two horses to spare—the palomino was for McMaster, the Appaloosa for Jerry. "You can ride?"

"Yes."

"Good, it isn't far, Reverend," McMaster smiled.

"We welcome you to freedom," said the crooked-nosed man on the chestnut mount. "My name's Jake. You've met McMaster already. This here's Jolene Arlen, and this man is Hoskins, the best sapper this side of the Mississippi. Carl Wall here is a tracker."

"Pleased," Jerry huffed, as he was helped into the saddle and handed the reins by McMaster.

Nobody moved. "Shouldn't we go?" Jeeters asked.

"In just a minute," Jake said. "You just look over at your TV tower there. Is it 12:26 yet, Reverend? What's that fancy watch of yor'n say?"

Jeeters looked at his luminous Rolex. "In another thirty seconds."

McMaster smiled. "Jake's right. We can spare a few seconds. Just watch the tower. We couldn't have a real collaborator take over your job now, could we, Reverend?"

Thirty seconds passed. On the thirty-first second, there was a series of small explosions at the base of the five-hundred-foot high structure. The broadcast tower slowly toppled over, falling in the direction of the Soviet troop barracks. When it hit, soldiers screamed and came out of the collapsed barracks firing wildly at the

9

darkness. Some were in their underwear, some naked.

"We'd better go now," Jake said. "Just wanted to see that." They rushed through the woods, the horses seemingly able to see the trees in the dark.

The cool wind of freedom seemed to caress the escapee's face. Freedom is like a long lost lover, Jeeters thought. A lover he had longed for, prayed for. And his prayers had been answered.

Chapter Two

"Mission accomplished," McMaster reported as he and Jeeters came through the flap into the old army tent. Jeeters saw the man at the desk — or should he say boy at the desk — look up. The minister was startled by the boy's appearance. One half of his face was totally burned away. That side was just a mass of red swells — no features. The other half — the left half — was a perfectly normal teenage face.

The boy's half-lips smiled. He stood up. "Glad to hear things went well," the boy said. "I'm Chris, the local elected chieftain of the Revengers. Titles don't matter much, though. I'm in charge here, and I welcome you."

Jeeters nodded. "Thanks." He shook hands. The boy's grip was hard. "I've heard a lot about you, Chris. The Reds are always complaining about the teenage 'snipe' who is harassing the hell out of the whole Appalachian region."

"I'm flattered. And I admire you too, Reverend. We've depended heavily on your coded messages over the years to plot our moves against the Soviets. You are a great hero to us, Reverend. That is, you are a hero to those Americans who know about your Bible code. (See C.A.D.S. #2.) How come you knew the Reds were on to you?"

"I had an informant," Jeeters said. "A good Russian who wanted his country to be peaceful. He was part of the Gorbachev faction that was purged just before the war. This man—Bukarnov—disappeared suddenly. I knew they were on to me, when they told me Bukarnov was 'reassigned.' I heard a casual remark in the cafeteria, that Bukarnov's relatives in the Soviet Union received a bill in the mail for the bullets used to shoot him. Possibly, I wasn't killed right off because Bukarnov, somehow, didn't tell on me, not even under torture. The Reds never did figure out how I was passing Bukarnov's intel on right under their noses. But they were analyzing my broadcasts. I knew that, because they suddenly asked for broadcast transcript copies. It was a matter of time . . ."

"I see," Chris said. "One more thing I'm curious about."

Jeeters realized that Chris was not just "curious." He was giving him a real debriefing. Plus, the young Revenger-chieftain was double checking that he truly was JJJ in the flesh, and not a Sov impersonator.

He answered a few more of the boy's questions, then said, "I know you have lots of questions, but I have to show you this secret report. It's the last thing Bukarnov gave me." Jerry dug the dog-eared document out of his inner left pocket. "Here, this is it."

Chris took it, and squinted at the print. "It's in Russian. I don't read Russkie."

Jeeters took it back and read it: "It says the Reds have bombed the western White House at White Sands base—the home base of the C.A.D.S. unit. The Soviets hit it with a germ bomb."

Everyone in the tent just stood in stunned silence. "Then all is lost!" Chris shook visibly. "The President; the C.A.D.S. unit; all gone! I was a close friend of

12

Robin Adler, the wife of Dean Sturgis, leader of the C.A.D.S. unit," Chris said. "She was like a mother to me, saved me — after N-Day . . ."

"This report," added Jeeters, "says that the C.A.D.S. unit wasn't there when the bomb hit."

"What?"

"According to this report, the C.A.D.S. unit was out in the desert somewhere," Jeeters said. He saw the relief spread over Chris's half-countenance. "The Reds can't verify if the President is really dead either. White Sands might have detected the bombers coming and sealed off in time. The whole base was deep underground!"

"Didn't the Sovs do a follow-up paradrop on the base?"

"No," Jeeters said, "The Sovs couldn't follow up with a paradrop. The weather was too bad. They don't know how effective the germ-bombing was. We can hope." Jeeters put the report on Chris's desk and added, "Did you hear about what happened in the Kremlin a few weeks ago?"

"Yes," Chris smiled. "The C.A.D.S. unit blew the hell out of it — and rescued Sturgis's wife Robin in the process. We monitor the Soviet signals. We have half their codes, thanks to you. We know that the Premier of Russia was killed by the C.A.D.S. unit, and that the Kremlin was wasted. Now there's a civil war going on in Russia for power — and the Sov occupation force here is on its own — with no back-up from Moscow. There are secret communiques from Moscow indicating they will take a while to get things in shape to run things from there again."

"The C.A.D.S. unit is heading for White Sands, according to latest Sov intel," Jeeters added. "For some reason Sturgis and his men didn't return to White Sands directly. They stopped in the desert a few hundred miles short of the base. But the last report from

Bukarnov indicates that the Reds are going to fire a nuke-tipped missile at White Sands soon. A coup-de-grâce!"

"We've got to warn the C.A.D.S. troopers not to go to White Sands," Jake said.

"How?" Chris replied. "We've got no communication with them." The boy pounded a fist on the desk in frustration.

"Then you have to *send* someone to warn them," Jeeters insisted. "We can't lose the C.A.D.S. unit!"

"Two thousand five hundred miles!" Chris shook his head. "We don't know exactly where the C.A.D.S. unit is located. We can't do it—"

"You've *got* to do it," Jeeters said waving his hand around like a preacher-in-action. "C.A.D.S. is America's last hope of actually defeating the Reds. All you Revengers can do is harass the shit out of them, deny them victory. But the Reds can't be defeated without C.A.D.S."

"Won't the C.A.D.S. unit's high-tech armor suits protect them?" Jake asked.

"Probably it'll protect them from any lingering germs," Chris reasoned, "but you heard what Jeeters said. A nuke missile attack will follow soon. Even C.A.D.S. couldn't stand a direct nuke-hit. No, we've got to keep them away from White Sands. We have to go there and warn them, *somehow.*"

"Yes," Jeeters said, "now you understand."

Chris sat back down heavily. "Get all the maps out, Jake, and call a meeting for one hour from now. Jeeters, I know you must be tired, but can you be at that meeting?"

"You bet." Jeeters admired the kid's decisiveness.

"One last question," Chris said. "How did the Reds know where the western White House was located? They would have bombed White Sands long ago, if it

14

could have been spotted from the sky."

Jeeters replied, "The Reds have an informant named Pinky Ellis, an American arch-traitor. Pinky knew of White Sands base for years, but for some reason only passed the exact location to the Reds a few weeks ago."

Chris looked out the tent flap at the white flowering mountain laurels. "Well, I'm sure you want some food and rest — we'll see you at the meeting. And, preacher, I think that it's time for you to get dressed like all of us."

"Oh that can wait," Jeeters said.

"I'm afraid not," Jake grimaced. "You see, Reverend, I have to tell you, most Americans consider *you* an arch-traitor. Maybe now that you're out safe, you can get the recognition you deserve for your patriotic acts. But until the word is passed, I think you'd better change your clothes. You don't want to be a target to your own side, do you? Everyone knows your face and your sissy clothes very well. We hear you spouting your pro-Red garbage mixed with Bible verses on TV every week!"

Jerry nodded, "Yes, of course — I should wear other clothes."

Chris smiled. "Get him some Revenger duds, Jake. And get me the you-know-what. I want to present it at the meeting in the crystal cave."

"Crystal cave?" Jeeters asked.

Chris nodded. "A safe place. The Reds will come a'looking for us soon. But we'll be long gone by then, into the crystal cave. Suffice to say there's a honeycomb of natural caves in the Appalachians that we've been connecting over the last nine or ten years. Safety from the Reds. A place to rest our bones and lick our wounds. We have hospitals, rec areas, the works — even a nursery. There are tons of kids. We try to keep the human race human, you know, by selective breeding."

"Then the fight against the Reds is going well!"

"Thanks to you it is — and of course thanks to the

C.A.D.S. unit. World War Three ain't over yet."

"Chris," Jeeters asked, "I want to come on the mission west with you."

Chris thought it over a moment, then nodded.

Once Jeeters left, Chris's eyes stared far off. He saw not the tent, but Robin Adler's face. Chris would never forget Robin.

Questions plagued him. Was she alive? Was Robin with her husband Dean Sturgis? Would the Revenger expedition be able to find the C.A.D.S. unit in time to stop their destruction?

The responsibility was great, and all on Chris's shoulders!

Chapter Three

At 1800 hours, the meeting convened in a small auditorium in the so-called crystal caves complex.

"These caves are amazing," exclaimed Jeeters. "Where is the light coming from? Are those fluorescent bulbs up there in the rock ceiling?"

Chris laughed. "Yes. We make power with a set of gasoline powered generators — mostly old eight-cylinder car engines. The fluorescent bulbs are among the supplies we 'liberated' from the Russian supply convoys we ambushed a few years back. Oh, the electric power is chancy. Don't be alarmed if we lose it from time to time."

Jeeters settled down into one of the theater-like chairs arranged in a semi-circle around a dais, which held a table and four oak chairs. The logo of the American eagle crushing the Soviet hammer-and-sickle in its claws in the middle of the dais attracted the preacher's eyes. It bore the words, "Freedom or death."

Jake, Chris, Carl, and McMaster took the seats up in front, and the twenty or so seats around the minister filled up with rugged mountain men — and four comely young ladies. Three of the latter were holding babies. One of the babies was sucking at an ample pink breast. The other two were bawling. Then they too were given mothers' milk. Jeeters blushed when one of the mothers caught him looking, and he averted his eyes.

On the way through the snaking tunnel that sloped down from the surface to the rock-hewn chamber, Jeeters had seen lots of babies. Chris hadn't been fooling when he said the Revenger group encouraged reproduction!

Chris stood up and waved everyone to silence. "Before we begin, I'd like to introduce our hero, Jerry Jeff Jeeters, whom you all now know wasn't a Red dupe at all, but an agent of the American resistance. Stand up Jerry, will ya?"

Jeeters, red-faced, rose up and gave a brief wave. There was loud applause and a few whistles. Chris opened a box he had placed up on the dais, stood up and approached Jeeters, holding forth the small object that he took from the box. The boy pinned it to Jeeters's new khaki jacket. "This is the Purple Oak Cluster, the highest award that goes to any American patriot."

More applause. When it died down, Chris told everyone that Carl and Jake needed a few minutes to get their material together, "so everyone should just relax for a spell."

Chris, when people started milling about, introduced Jeeters to one of the prettiest women he'd ever seen. The strawberry blond, silken haired, turquoise-eyed beauty was one of the three young women in the audience who were holding babies. When called over by Chris, she pushed past several seats and just stood in front of the reverend and smiled shyly.

"This filly's name is Cat," Chris said, "and the big boy baby she's holding is Dean Harrison Sturgis."

"You mean—"

"Yes," Cat said, "This here brat is Dean Sturgis's boy-child. He visited here, a little over three years ago and left me with this cute little present growing in my gut.

18

Big, isn't he? Little Dean here will be two years, six months old next week! He's my pride and joy."

Jeeters smiled. "He is cute." The reverend couldn't help noticing that Cat was very pregnant again. He didn't ask who the father was, but he didn't have to ask. Brazenly, Cat said, "Chris here is the father of my child-to-be." She proudly thrust a grape-sized diamond ring into Jeeters's face. "How's that engagement stone?"

"Large . . ." Jeeters said, not knowing exactly how to respond.

"We'd better get on with the meeting," Chris said. "They seem to be ready now."

They all took their seats again and Chris ascended the stage and banged a carpenter's ball hammer on the table to stop all the chatter around the room. "Carl, can you show us the maps?"

The grizzly-sized thickly gray-bearded man brought up a long blue cylinder with tripod attached. He set it down alongside the podium and pulled up a rod, opening up the first map. It was an old high school history class map of the United States, showing terrain, not state boundaries. There were many added nota- tions — black solid lines, dotted red lines, blue and green triangles. Battle lines.

Chris took up a stick and pointed to a spot in the Appalachian mountain chain. "Here we are," he said. "And these added notations you see are the Soviet fortresses and supply depots — the green triangles. And our strongholds are the blue ones."

"It ain't up to date," someone in the audience re- marked aloud, "most of that stuff's from a survey done a year ago."

"Men died to get that info," Carl snapped back, breaking a pencil in his beefy hands. "You don't tell me it 'ain't much'."

"No arguments," Chris insisted. "Now just pay attention." He pointed the stick to a winding dotted red line. "This is the trail I suggest we use to go west. We use our horses to this point in Ohio, and from there, we use the old Interstate. We bring some mechanics and some batteries. McMaster says we can resurrect some cars we find out there, fix 'em up for overland travel at great speed. It's been done before. The batteries are the one part our guys can't fix, so we bring 'em along."

"How about the horses?" Carson asked. "Once we get cars, what do we do with our horses?"

Chris shrugged. "We can let 'em graze till we return."

"How about hostiles?" McMaster said. "Been a while since anyone has been out in those parts."

"We know that there are patriot-bands that will help us along the way to Ohio. After Ohio, well . . ." Chris trailed off. Everyone looked uneasy and Jeeters heard whispers about "Savages . . . cannibals . . ."

Chris went on. "We reach the Mississippi here, near this bend, and hit this small Sov base. Get some supplies. And then head directly toward White Sands."

"How many men do we take?" It was a cold-eyed blond young man asking the question. He wore a pork-pie hat and cradled a shotgun.

"Twenty-five, maybe thirty." Chris replied. "Including you, Deke."

"And how the hell do we find the C.A.D.S. unit out there—even if they are near White Sands?" Deke spoke out again.

"If all goes well, we'll get close and they'll pick up our signal—we bring a small transmitter."

Deke shook his head. "Too many 'ifs', Chris."

"The C.A.D.S. unit can scan for miles with their high-tech gear," Chris retorted. "They'll pick up our signal. We have to hope, though, that they don't shoot the hell out of us. Look," Chris said, exasperation edging his voice, "this plan is not ironclad guaranteed.

Anybody have a better plan?"

"How 'bout we forget the whole thing," a grizzled old codger rose to say. "We can't make that journey in less than a month. I say that we will be too late."

There were murmurs of agreement.

"We have to try," Chris said. "You don't have to come, Johnston."

"Can we take a vote?" Deke insisted. "To know where we stand."

They did take a vote, and Johnston was the only one who didn't raise his hand when Chris made the motion that they mount the expedition as he had outlined.

"That settles that," Chris said.

Jeeters was amazed at how quickly and effectively the meeting went after that troubled start. Experts in every field of endeavor now came up and spoke about the details of the operation, what they would need to bring, and so on. It was all worked out in a matter of hours. One interesting note was when Chris proposed that someone named F-Stop come along "to document this expedition for the future." F-Stop Fitzgerald was a photographer, it seemed.

Chris was smart, Jerry realized. Smart and aware of everything! No wonder he was the head honcho at such an early age. And this town-meeting proved democracy was alive and well. Jeeters had no doubts now. Not after seeing Chris handle this meeting! They'd make it!

"We leave at 0600 hours tomorrow," Chris said. "Be ready at the main cave entrance. No more than five pounds of personal gear each. You know, bring only your lucky charms, notepads and so on. Nothing frivolous."

"How about booze?" McMaster commented. "That ain't frivolous."

"Long as it's under five pounds worth. That's about two liters, McMaster."

"Ain't nearly enough," the man complained.

Everyone laughed.

That night, Jeeters was given a small room of his own deep inside the cave complex. He was again amazed on the way to his bedroom, for the long winding natural passage that he was led along was breathtaking. The corridor was lined with crystal quartz formations, exquisite jewel-like formations that he could never even have dreamed about. McMaster, who led him along at a stiff pace, told him, "Now you know how this place got its name, Jeeters. We used to call the whole complex 'Camp X,' but all these crystals made us change the name."

Jeeters lay back on the cool fresh linen of his ample feather bed and stared at a crystalline ceiling above. But only for a short while. He was very tired. He drifted off to sleep with the image of that baby suckling at Cat's breast in his mind's eye.

Hours later, there was a soft knock at his door. Barely enough to wake him. He glanced at his luminous dial Big Ben alarm clock. Four A.M. "Come in," he said, yawning. The reverend was expecting some military type, rousing him to begin packing. But it wasn't a guy at all. It was a beautiful woman. It was the woman who had been sitting two seats from him at the meeting; the raven-haired woman that had made it hard for him to listen to the talk, because of her great beauty.

"Hi," she whispered, closing and locking the door. "I'm Beth. Remember me?"

"Sure," the reverend said, sitting up and pulling the sheet up a bit. He slept in the raw. The young raven-haired beauty was wearing a nightie — just a nightie — and her feet were bare. She smiled warmly. "My room is right next to yours. It gets very lonely, so I thought

22

I'd join you—okay?"

"I don't know if I—"

"Oh you *should*," she said, slipping under the sheet and pressing her full, warm body against his, "I'm the only one of the technicians in this section who isn't pregnant yet. You look very fertile. Would you mind doing me this one little bitty favor? Just tonight?" She almost cooed her request.

The reverend's resolution was not as stiff as his manly tool was at that moment, and she was a *tiger*. She mounted him, her sex wet and insistent, and before he could protest—if he was going to do that at all—Beth had fit tightly down onto him. Then started a wild ride. "Oh, this feels so good," she moaned. "Thank you, thank you."

"M—My pleasure," the reverend gasped out. "B—Be my guest!"

After an hour of repeated genetic improvement, the girl left Jerry Jeff Jeeters. Eventually, the reverend recovered and dressed. He put on his new brown army helmet, and his khakis, and stared in the mirror. There was quite a change in his face, as well as in his outfit. The change of expression was Beth's doing. He liked the khaki and the helmet, and his new relaxed expression a lot, and Jeeters decided not to shave. He liked the stubble on his face too! Maybe he'd find a cheroot somewhere and chew on it, to complete the new macho-image. Jeeters whistled as he left the room. Life was already much more interesting than it had been back at the Sov broadcast station. And a heck of a lot more pleasurable.

Chapter Four

Far to the West:

The tents erected at the edge of Utah's Great Salt Lake were large, striped affairs. They looked like they belonged at an oasis in the Sahara, not in Utah. But there were no camels tethered outside these billowing tents. Instead, a convoy of weather- and grime-worn war-vehicles, heavily armored, bristling with weapons, were parked a short distance away. Some of the vehicles were modified school buses, their yellow paint covered with brown and gray camouflage. Some were jeeps, their windshields replaced with heavy boiler plate with a few gun slits. A few of the thirty vehicles were converted RV's. Big-tired high-off-the-terrain jobbies. A post-nuke armada for overland travel.

There was one pleasure vehicle among all the grim war-armaments. Near the largest tent—a fifty-foot by sixty-foot sized affair—was parked a shiny white Rolls Royce. The vehicle belonged to the "boss," a warlord who managed to live a life of opulence amid the ruins of nuked-out America. A man who took his creature comforts seriously.

There was music pouring from the open flap of the boss's tent: "Unchained Melody," by Al Hibbler. It was an old scratchy recording on a plastic disk. The kind of music reproduction system that had once been called "a record."

The two gaunt tall men wading in the edge of the great lake, despite being a hundred yards away, could hardly hear themselves think over the strains of music, and they didn't like it. Their boss had played that song over and over again, until they were nearly nuts from hearing it. But they didn't complain. They had seen what happened to men that gave backtalk to the three-hundred-and-seventy-five-pound tub of lard who ran their operation. They had to let their boss, Pinky Ellis, play his music whenever he wanted. Because Pinky was their meal ticket, he was their way of living, of staying alive in a world gone to hell!

The two men in the sun, wading with their khaki pants rolled up to their thighs, didn't much like the job they had been assigned to do this sunny morning. They were fishing. Fishing the post-apocalypse way. And they weren't supposed to stop fishing until they caught something for Pinky's lunch.

The bald one suddenly stopped wading. "Freeze, Martino. I see a fish!"

Martino stopped wading and watched Levinsky carefully unsling his smg from around his shoulder and aim it at the water between them. A little too close to Martino's feet for comfort. "Hey, Levinsky," Martino said softly, "you're not gonna—"

His words were cut off by the burst of fire from Levinsky's weapon.

When the smaller man wiped the salt water from his eyes, he saw a large catfish had floated up to the surface, a catfish nearly cut in half by bullet holes.

"Hot damn, I got it," Levinsky shouted.

"You nearly got me too, you bastard!" Martino said as he lunged for the other man. They fell into the water, struggling, clutching one another's throat.

25

Then came a booming voice—Pinky's voice. Evidently he had looked over with his binoculars when he heard the shots. "That's enough!" Pinky yelled out through the battery-driven bullhorn. "Bring that fish to the mess tent. Then go back to your regular duties."

Pinky put the bullhorn back down on the blue sand beside the canvas beach chair he lounged in. He sighed, thinking about the taste of fresh trout. Or swordfish. Or halibut with cream sauce—and some endives and some—. Well, catfish was *something* anyway. Cookie would know what to do with it. He would know what to do to make it taste *French*. Post-nouvelle cuisine was his specialty. Catfish his tour-de-force.

Still, I'd rather have a Mrs. Paul's flounder fillet, Pinky thought. The catfish in this lake had a peculiar odor and taste. Sort of like the catfish all ate something long dead. They probably did. About the only species alive in America now were those that could eat either their own kind or could feed on something long dead!

Pinky's little beach was very small, just ten feet of bluish sand. In both directions from his chair the edge of the lake was not sand, but rather a strange, hard pale green substance. Except for this patch, it had been turned into green glass by the action of a nuclear bomb. The bomb that had taken out Salt Lake City and all its inhabitants a few years back. And left this beachfront property *uncrowded*.

Pinky's huge blubbery girth was covered with sun tan lotion, Strength 16, and he had on a pair of pointy-edge rhinestone-encrusted women's sun glasses. One lens was cracked, but the lenses afforded protection for his sensitive pale blue eyes. He had to make do. Supplies were getting hard to come by now, so many years after N-Day. That was why he was heading north, toward a place that Pinky was sure would provide all the supplies he needed. And more. But he didn't like to rush. A few days here on the beach would not hurt. He needed the time to cool out, to relax and forget Morgana Pinter, who was dead now anyway. Dead because she and all her loyalist friends at White Sands had been betrayed by the Commies' best friend in America; betrayed by Pinky.

Ah yes, he thought, *the Communists*. They were truly magnificent! He would mount a feast tonight, in their honor. Then perhaps he should order his little band to move onward. To claim their new home. The feast tonight would be dedicated to all of the Soviet generals who were his good friends now. Dedicated to his comrades, his powerful and clever comrades! Maybe he would have the moose in the refrigerator-truck thawed and roasted on a spit. Yes, that sounded lovely. After a light lunch of catfish, it would be nice to have something a bit more *hearty* for supper!

It was a lovely night, not too cool, and the sky was clear and full of stars. The feast was held outdoors, between the tents. Pinky's fat face was lit up by the many flaming torches erected alongside the set of picnic tables. He stood before his top officers. The orange torchlight lit up his chubby face as Pinky raised his champagne glass. "I give a toast," Pinky said, "to all of the great ones. I toast Veloshnikov, Supreme Marshal Veloshnikov, a man of many victories and more to come. I raise a toast to all our Russian friends."

"Hear, hear," his traitorous gang responded, raising their full-to-the-brim glasses in response. "To the Russians!"

Pinky drank his glass to the bottom, some champagne running down his chin and dripping on his pink and white striped tailored shirt. The shirt had been made by the same man who had designed the tents. He

27

cursed and wiped at the spill with a napkin. At least, Pinky thought, I haven't spilled on my tuxedo!

His men, not so elegantly dressed as their leader, didn't mind that the drinks might spill on their pirate-like outfits or on their filthy beards. They were just glad to be drinking and eating. The braised moose was delicious, even if it was *just a little bit* radioactive.

Pinky glanced at his watch. "Hey," he shouted. "Why didn't someone tell me that it's time for the Jerry Jeff Jeeters Gospel Hour?"

Everyone tried to look elsewhere, to not meet his glaring eyes.

"Never mind," Pinky said, "we only missed a minute!" Pinky was the only one allowed to touch the battery powered Sony TV set. He went over to the table outside his tent where it rested — under heavy guard — and turned it on. The image came on slowly, the battery was low. But in a minute the color TV picture was there. But it wasn't the appealing face of the Bible thumper that Pinky saw on the twelve-inch screen. Instead, there was just the station logo — a cross super-imposed with a hammer and sickle. The announcer's voice came on, first in Russian, which Pinky knew little of, and then repeating in English: "Due to technical difficulties the Jerry Jeff Jeeters show will not be seen tonight. Instead we will have a program of Soviet martial music."

"Martial music sucks!" Pinky snapped. He turned the set off and strode into his tent. Soon the camp resounded with the scratchy record they all hated so very very much: "Unchained Melody."

Inside his luxury tent, Pinky shooed all his servants away. He had hoped to find some solace in the Jeeters show. But now he just wanted to be alone. He had, despite his best efforts, been missing Morgana. The strains of the song came on and Pinky sighed. He had hated telling the Sovs about White Sands base, because Morgana was there. He had wanted her back for so long that he just went crazy one day and decided if he couldn't have her—no one else could. So he had squealed the location of the U.S. base to the Sovs. The C.A.D.S. unit and the old U.S. government at White Sands had been a thorn in his side anyway. But damn it, he missed Morgana. Missed humiliating and torturing her. He especially missed her tears.

He fell asleep sobbing out her name.

Chapter Five

"Boss," Levinsky shouted, "Boss wake up! Someone's comin'." The aide continued to shake Pinky Ellis. It was sort of like shaking a huge bowl of pink jelly, the anxious subordinate thought, and he smiled nervously, then repressed the smile. He musn't *ever* think bad thoughts about Pinky Ellis, his warlord, his boss, his meal ticket.

Pinky, after repeated shakings, finally groaned and he opened one bloodshot eye. "What the frigging hell is it? What time is it anyway?"

"It's just after dawn, boss. Sorry to wake you but you said to wake you if somebody comes our way."

"What?"

"Yeah, Boss; there's smoke and dust on the horizon. And—"

"Why didn't you say so?" Pinky, throwing on a pink silk kimono specially enlarged for his use, bounded out of his feather bed and rushed to the entrance of the tent. He grabbed the Questar telescope, a powerful device he had had more than one occasion to use in the past. One problem with the Questar was that the damned thing was an astronomical telescope, so the image was presented upside down! Still, it was a clear image.

"Vector thirty west, boss," Levinsky said.

"I've got it," Pinky snarled, as he focused in on a group of vehicles twenty miles away. Dancing and bending in the morning heat Pinky saw three large trucks, all bristling with guns. And there were at least a dozen motorcycles with sidecars, with passengers and drivers wearing goggles and dressed all in white. The big Harleys each had racks of mini-missiles on their fronts.

Behind the caravan of well-armed cycles and trucks was a luxury four door sedan. A low slung Italian job of some sort. "My God!" Pinky exclaimed, as a truck veered a bit and gave him a good view, "There's a fire-engine-red Lamborghini in that convoy!"

"What's a Lamborghini, boss?"

"Low-life stupido! It is the most expensive Italian sports car there is—was! The leader of that group," Pinky said slyly, "must be a man after my own taste. Someone classy and well educated is riding in that car." Pinky became silent, continuing to stare through the powerful telescope.

"They must be close enough to see us now, boss." Levinsky said. "Should I do what we always do when an armed party approaches us? Should I lob a few mortars at them? Warn them off?"

Pinky said nothing. He was engrossed in staring through the scope.

It made Levinsky nervous to think that an armed group was coming so close. "Should I send out some of our men, boss? Face them down and demand their food and—"

"No," Pinky said, "I have a gut feeling that we might want to talk to them on a friendly basis. Send out a man in a jeep under a white flag. No, better yet, go yourself. Invite their leader to come and lunch with me. And with you of course, Levinsky."

31

Levinsky gulped hard and then saluted. He walked away with trepidation. More than once he'd seen a man under a white flag be blown to shit. In post-nuke America, a truce flag didn't mean a whole lot. He wondered if he would be alive for lunch.

The leader of the approaching group had, to Levinsky's great relief, accepted the offer for lunch. As the main body of the strange entourage stayed out a distance from Pinky's lakeside camp, the red Lamborghini with a phalanx of the 'cycles around it approached their tents.

Pinky had his Al Hibbler record on again, and lounged on a dozen fat pillows next to a sumptuous spread of food. The red sports car pulled up and the motor was cut off. Pinky squinted to see who was inside the car, but the windows were opaque. He sat up and watched as the chauffeur came around and opened the rear door of the car. Pinky held his breath. For a long time no one stepped out. Then Pinky saw a ruby jeweled high heeled shoe appear under the door, and a fat ankle above it. Then he saw the jeweled red stockings. A *woman!* The leader of the new group was a woman!

Finally, the massiveness of *her* appeared and Pinky nearly fainted in awe. Oh, the sheer beautiful mass of her! Who was this ample goddess of the desert? It was love at first sight!

When the goddess turned her chubby face in his direction Pinky stuttered out, "W-who — who are you?"

"I am Anetra, Lady of Atlantis, leader of the Cult of the White Light, queen of the upper and lower kingdom, heiress to the wisdom of the ages. And I am, of course, also the reincarnation of Venus, goddess of Love. — And who are you, my fair and ample handsome knight?"

Pinky said, "I am — your most thankful admirer and your host. I am Pinky Ellis, God's shadow on earth, lord of the desert and the mountains. Please accept my hospitality, great one." He went to her, in a sort of stagger, and Pinky fell at Anetra's feet and clutched at her knees.

She smiled down at him, "You are so polite. I am pleased to accept your invitation."

Pinky kissed her extended hands and each of her ten ringed fingers. He rose up and then they stared into each other's eyes — for a long time. "Destiny has brought you here, brought us together," Pinky said. "I knew you were Venus the minute you stepped from the shell of your great car. You came out of the Lamborghini like you used to come out of the sea shell in all those old paintings. Venus, I bow to you."

What is this shit? Levinsky thought. Why is the boss kowtowing to that fat broad? She looks more like Miss Piggy than any Venus!

Levinsky watched the boss lead the fat broad to the table and hold her chair out for her. Called over, he poured their wine and listened to the dame say, "Excellent wine. You are a very tasteful and intelligent man, Pinky Ellis — and so handsome!" Levinsky nearly puked as the fat ones wrapped their arms around each other and drank from each other's cup.

"Most women are too thin nowadays, don't you think?" Pinky said. "They have no substance . . ."

"Indeed I do think so," Anetra agreed. "It is a privilege to be in the company of a nobleman who understands beauty is not — skimpy." She fluttered her eyelids.

Levinsky was *sure* he would puke now. Fortunately,

33

the boss told him to go put the record back on again and wind up the old phonograph once more. So he was able to get out of sight of the fat couple. Levinsky wondered if something was beginning here that would turn out badly for him and the other men. They all depended on the cruelty and ruthlessness of the boss to get them through the world. If the boss started acting like a pussycat, they were all in danger!

After lunch, Pinky and Anetra left their men — Pinky had invited her whole entourage to the camp — to mingle and make friends. And they went off alone, holding hands, to the nearby hills, which were covered with wildflowers. They danced through the waist high flowers, bounding seemingly weightlessly along together. Anetra was resplendent in her gossamer ruby jeweled gown, and Pinky had changed into his red jogging outfit. They were like schoolkids in love for the first time.

As they reclined in one another's arms at a babbling brook, Pinky said, "Together, my love, we shall rule the multitudes, build a better world."

"Yes, my love," she said, "yes." Their voluminous lips met, and dripping saliva over each other, they tongue-kissed for hours.

Later, in the tent, the new lovers talked of weightier matters: "We must plan our future, my darling," Pinky said. "I am headed for a great underground fort, a powerful base from which the world can be ruled. I ask you to come with me, and share my power."

"Yes," she moaned. "Together we shall rule."

"I will ask the men to pack up, and your men as well. We must, alas, move on tonight. Fort Collins awaits us.

34

And with the power of that vast fortress we can—"

Anetra finished for him, as she placed a grape on his tongue. "We can rule the world," she smiled. "I will never be away from your side."

Pinky swallowed the grape and then he turned and shouted through the tent flap, "Levinsky! Put 'Unchained Melody' on again! And after that, play 'Sound of Music.' "

The Al Hibbler hit came on as he put another kumquat to her lips and she placed a raw oyster in Pinky's mouth. They chewed together, staring into each other's smitten eyes.

Chapter Six

They were nearly upon White Sands base, and the C.A.D.S. unit should have heard the identity-challenge code on their channel 32. But the airwaves were as silent as the desert.

As the metal-armored men of the fabled Omega command—or what was left of them after many battles—passed between two tall pillars of sandstone, the wind's howl was a mournful sound, like a coyote in distress. It was a scary desolate sound that seemed to say, "ahead is nothing but death."

Each man, distrustful of the battered systems of their computerized battle armor, had accessed a different mode, so that none would depend on all systems functioning.

Tranh Van Noc, second in command of the unit, had his visor on clear mode, so he could look into the face plate of his commander, Dean Sturgis. He saw the grim set of his commander's jaw, and the dread in his steel gray eyes. The Vietnamese-American approached his commander and they touched helmets together, to speak without the others overhearing. Tranh said, "I don't like the feeling I'm getting, Skip. Have you noticed the wind is always coming from White Sands base? Even when we circled north a bit to avoid that crevasse, the wind shifted. It seems to always come from the base."

"What do you suppose causes it?"

Tranh replied, "I don't have any idea. But I think it could be a surface phenomena — say a wind pattern set up by a hole in the ground. A large new hole."

"You think they've been hit?"

Before Tranh could reply, the answer came up on the colonel's computer projected displays: *"Warning.* Bacteriological contamination ahead. Secure helmets. Initiating G-sequence."

Sturgis was bone tired, and he had to ask the computer, "What the hell is G-sequence?"

The readout in his helmet advised, "G-sequence is decontamination. C.A.D.S. units surfaces are being sterilized."

As Sturgis read the computer print, he felt a rising heat. He was amazed to see that his right metal glove was glowing a bright cherry red. The glow rapidly advanced to all the other parts of his metal armor then disappeared with a hissing sound. "G-sequence complete," the readout reported.

"What the hell is going on, Skip?" It was their mechanical whiz, Mickey Rossiter's voice. Rossiter had the worst, most battered suit of the bunch, because he was the best at patching them. "God," Rossiter said, "I was almost fried. Who knew there was even such a function in the suits?"

"Are you all right?" Sturgis asked.

Mickey said, "Think so, Skip. Though I know what a chicken feels like on a rotisserie now. Does this mean that White Sands Base really has been germ-bombed?"

"Yeah, Skip," added a voice with a southern drawl — Billy Dixon. The platinum blond southern boy added, "my suit is a half-wrecked old model with rocket dents on it. Half my circuits say there's danger ahead, half say there isn't. It's very stuffy in here. Skip, can't I open up?"

Several other voices joined in on the radio, all saying that their readouts were confusing, and asking how to proceed.

Sturgis ordered, "Stay sealed, all of you! Believe the half of your readouts that say *danger*. That's the general rule. Now form up; we're going in on full alert, sealed and ready for battle."

They stormed over the hill, like gleaming black titans from another planet, their steel cleats making deep gouges in the desert's hard packed soil as they approached at thirty miles per hour, super-running toward their home base. Heading toward the only place on earth any one of them could call home.

And they found only devastation. A huge circular gouge in the desert floor a hundred meters wide, with a bluish smoke rising from it. And smashed machinery and pieces of human bodies were all strewn about that hole.

Billy fell to his knees, *"No,"* he gasped out, "No, not the President; not our friends! They can't be gone!" He began to weep, and then he started to struggle with the emergency clamps of his helmet, attempting to open up and breath in the blue gas floating about in the air.

Fenton grabbed his arms and held them back. "No, Billy, don't do that. The hole isn't all the way down to the last levels of the base. There could still be someone alive there."

Billy Dixon tore his friend's arms away with a sparking of metal on metal. "You're just saying that, Fenton," he ejaculated. "There's no one left alive in here— They're all dead. Ain't it obvious from all those germs! That blue cloud is germs! My computer says so!"

Sturgis realized that Billy, one of the toughest fighters in the unit, was on the verge of hysteria. And why not? Nothing but fighting and death for years—and now this! He had to do something, fast. "Billy, snap out of it, get up!" Sturgis snarled. "That's an order Billy. Get hold of yourself."

Billy didn't stand up, and he didn't stop raving either. "All cooped up in this coffin-suit and there ain't nowhere to go. There's no more food, no more President, no more—"

Sturgis used the officer com-override to cut off Billy's transmissions. At least the others didn't have to hear this! But he kept his com to the southerner open. "Billy! Get hold of yourself. Do something useful! —Listen, your rocket pack has the most fuel of all of the suits. Jet out over the center of the crater. Get a readout on how deep that hole is before you pronounce the President's obituary. *Do it!*"

Sturgis watched the young man slowly rise, and then turn and salute. "Will do, Skip," he said in a weak voice.

Billy ignited his rocket pack and flames shot him up one-hundred feet and outward over the center of the fifty foot wide crater.

"Well, Billy? What do you see?" Sturgis asked.

Through heavy static, Billy reported, "Skip, the hole is down to D level—no deeper. I don't detect life forms on Blue or Red Mode."

"The shielding would prevent that, Billy." Sturgis said convincingly. "Come on down, I swear to you we'll find people alive in there."

"Yes," Billy said excitedly, "they might have covered up in time."

When Billy had returned to the crater's edge, Sturgis ordered a sweep of the area to find the source of any remaining germ-contaminants. Fenton soon shouted out, "Skip, there's some split cannisters over here on the south quadrant. My readout indicates it's anthrax,

39

some form of bloody anthrax germs. These cannisters are the source of the blue mist. I'm torching it now with the liquid plastic fire."

Sturgis and the others watched on telemode and saw the flames leap from Fenton's right arm. Soon the British trooper reported "Germs-zero." The warning lights slowly faded in their systems.

"Now," Sturgis said, "as soon as the blue mist dissipates, we go down in that crater and knock. According to all indications, there's no Sov soldiers around. There's nobody at all out there in the desert for miles. Not even a grasshopper or a coyote."

"Nothing *alive*," Tranh corrected.

"Yeah," the commander said. He waited three minutes until air quality was normal and said, "Well, let's go."

They used their belt line ropes to descend into the smoking crater. Sturgis, going down first, came upon red blotches in the sand. He aimed the analyzer at it and reported, "This is dried blood. A trail of it. It leads down to that steel plating—that appears to be a seal-door."

"Shall we try to pry the door open?" Fireheels asked.

Sturgis shook his helmet from side to side. "No time, Joe. The germs are gone, 'Inactive' says my computer. I say we open the door up real quick. They could be suffocating in there. We blast our way in and see if anyone's alive."

"Right!" Billy exclaimed. He could never stand delays.

Sturgis ordered his men to concentrate .30 mm shell fire on the edges of the steel plate door. Before he ordered them to fire, he paused to say a little silent prayer. He wondered: Would they find horrid decayed bodies inside? Would there be staring open-eyed corpses, their faces frozen in gasps of death?

40

"Commence firing," he said softly.

Even in their insulated battle suits, the men could hear and feel the tremendous blasts. The steel door came open with a resounding boom.

"Cease fire," Sturgis shouted. They were engulfed now in an immense dust cloud, which even their I.R. sensors couldn't penetrate for a few seconds. Then they saw a corridor, scarred with blast lines. And down that corridor, Sturgis saw some lights flickering.

"Good work, men. That does it! Billy, Fenton, help me pull this wreckage away and then we go in."

One at a time they entered the silent corridor of D level. They immediately came upon a few bodies, clumped together. "God, Skip, did we—" Billy began.

Sturgis turned one wide-eyed middle-aged woman's body over with a boot. "No, Billy. These people died from the germ attack. This level wasn't sealed off quickly enough. We should go down another level. There's probably no danger from the anthrax anymore, but stay sealed."

They found a hatch and pried it open, climbed down the ladder one level to a sealed door. Sturgis's metal hand slammed against the lock to force it open, and they came out onto level E. — And there were no lights.

Billy reported, "Hey, my boot brushed something. Shine your strobe over here, Fireheels," Billy asked, "mine is on the blink."

The glaring light revealed another wide-eyed body. "God, this is Mannes, one of the President's personal guards!" Fireheels exclaimed. "He was a good man."

"Yeah. And a hero," Sturgis said. "Look at his finger-nails. And the bloody marks over by the hatch door we just opened. Mannes used his last strength to seal this section off."

Billy was elated. "Then—the President could still be alive."

"There's a chance," Sturgis said. "Just a chance. — Tranh, you have the best analyzer. How's the germ count here?"

"Okay, Skip. It's all dissipated," the Vietnamese-accented voice said.

They climbed back out through the emergency access tunnel and went down another level. The door was sealed there too. "This is the lowest level," Sturgis said. "If they're not alive in here, there's no place they could have run, except the test-range caves."

"Bloody hell," Fenton said. "The caves have air vents on the surface! They'd be contaminated!"

"Well, here goes nothing," Sturgis said. He shoved the door off its hinges and stepped out into a dark chamber. When Fireheels hit the maxi-strobe, they saw a dusty disordered scene. Equipment strewn about; piles of cartons and barrels. And on the Ampli-mode the colonel heard a muffled cough.

"Someone's alive!" he whispered.

Hold it right there! A man said, jumping up from behind the piles of cartons with a sten-gun in his hand. Other khaki clad men also appeared now, and each held a weapon handy. The C.A.D.S. unit was confronted by a dozen armed men. Not Russians. Americans.

"Hey, it's me." Sturgis said on his amplimode. "Don't you recognize our outfits?"

"Maybe it's Americans in those suits, maybe it's not," the lead gunner snarled. "How do we know you're Americans? Just because you speak English?"

"Well, I don't really know the winners of the last five World Series, if that's what you want," Sturgis said, frowning. "But you might as well believe me. You know as well as I do that bullets don't do much damage to these suits!" Sturgis studied the man's face and recognized it. "Dexter, you meathead! Don't you recognize my voice? Who was it that beat you at arm wrestling three times in a row!"

"Sturgis? Is it really you?" Dexter coughed. "Colonel, what took you so long?" He lowered his weapon and the others did also. "For God's sake, Dean," the dirty-faced man said, "de-opaque your helmet visor! We were sure you were Reds."

The colonel said, "I'll go you one better than that!" He quickly undid his helmet snaps and removed the headpiece entirely. Sturgis recognized the man next to Dexter now as well. The youth had grown a beard, as curly a beard as his black hair. "Martel! It's you!"

"Yeah, it's me," the young electronics whiz said. "Alive and kicking. The grub hasn't been too good in here. Do you guys have any decent food?"

"K-ration from the Soviet Union, some Indian tribal versions of Mars bars. But later for that. Who made it through?"

Martel said, "The President is alive, but he's wounded, and sick. He is on an I.V. . . . Quartermain is dead, so is Gridley, but the rest of the cabinet — Burns and Turner — made it."

"Morgana?" Sturgis asked.

"She's fine, Dean. Your girlfriend was in the lowest level sleeping. The Reds hit us late at night. The blast took out mostly empty labs and stuff. You know the layout. Someone upstairs was a hero, and sealed off the —"

"The hero," Sturgis said, "was Mannes. We found his body."

"And the germs," Martel said, "are they all —"

"They are dissipated," Mickey chimed in. "You think we'd open up our suits if they weren't?"

"How about the rest of your crew, Dean?" Dexter asked. "Is Sheila, and Wosyck —"

"Dead," Sturgis said. "We had plenty of casualties."

Martel said, "I guess we should be happy to see any

43

of you. We thought you all had been killed. What's happening in the world out there?"

"I'll tell you all once I tell President Williamson! For God's sake," Sturgis said, "lead me to the President. I have an urgent report!"

Chapter Seven

The word of the C.A.D.S. unit's arrival at the decimated White Sands base spread quickly among the eighty-seven survivors. Sturgis never got a chance to see the President alone. Instead, by the time Sturgis was led into the hospital room, it was already loaded with occupants. The remaining cabinet members, plus Van Patten, the R and D man, and Zapata, one of the dead CIA chief Quartermain's close assistants, were all there.

Sturgis was not happy to see these men gathered around Williamson's bed. He'd had run-ins with all of them before. The lanky Oklahoman chief-of-state and Sturgis had made their peace, after many squabbles. But tow-headed General Burns and slack-jawed Admiral Turner—the Acid Duo—were another matter. Turner had called Sturgis "insane" more than once, and Burns once forced the courtmartial of Sturgis as a traitor! (See CADS #3.)

The young blonde nurse turned up the lights and then pressed a button, raising the upper part of the President's bed. She fluffed the gray-faced man's pillow. Sturgis thought the President was asleep. But Williamson opened his eyes now and smiled wanly.

"He just came off the respirator," Nurse Peters whispered to Sturgis, "we keep it nearby. Give him the oxygen-mouthpiece if he should begin to cough." She indicated where the device was located, to the left of the bed. Sturgis nodded.

The President focused on the colonel, and said, "Sturgis! Glad to see you. Get over here! Shake hands."

When Sturgis extended his hand, the President fumbled around before he took it and held it. "My damned eyes are on the blink! I want to make sure it really is you, Colonel." The President raised his other hand and felt around the colonel's face, and smiled, "Yes. I remember this scar on your chin and your features. They say I might get back my eyesight any day now. Can't you get that nurse out of here! The one that fusses over me so much!"

"I'll go," she said, "but I'll be back soon, you old fool."

Sarah Peters, before she left, whispered to Sturgis how sorry she was about Sheila DeCamp's loss, and then added, "Ten minutes. Then the President *must* rest again!"

"What's the situation?" President Williamson asked.

Everyone looked at Sturgis, anxiously. He was glad he'd had time to shower, shave and put on a new pair of black coveralls. Still, the looks stayed disapproving, even when the colonel said, "Moscow Mission accomplished."

Van Patten was first of the disapprovers to speak. The tall lean gray-haired scientist took the dead Meerschaum pipe from his dry lips and said, "Did you kill the Soviet Premier?"

"I *said* mission accomplished!" Sturgis repeated. "We just had a little trouble on the way back. Had to bail out of a stolen bomber, and it took a while to make our way back here. Fifty percent casualties."

The President pushed himself up a bit on his pillow and smiled at Sturgis. "Good job, Colonel! I just knew,"

46

he said proudly, "that you'd succeed."

Sturgis leaned over the bed. "Mr. President, it is true that the Kremlin is a wasted mass of rubble. *But,* as you have noticed, the Reds are not finished yet. I think we had better evacuate this base. Before it takes another hit."

"Ha!" General Burns cut in. Redfaced, he scoffed, "And where in hell do you expect us to evacuate *to,* Colonel?"

"I've found a place," Sturgis said. "I've inspected it briefly. It's called Ft. Collins. Another underground fortress."

"Really?" Turner said, "Where?" There was a tone of mockery in his voice.

"Back along the way we came. A few hundred miles. "It's a vast, untouched facility."

"Not on any of my maps," Burns said, pulling up the single chair and sitting down on it backward. "Maybe you got a little sand in your ears out there in the desert, Colonel. When your botched operation lost all those men and equipment." His blue eyes flared in hatred of the colonel.

"What do you mean to say, Burns? You don't believe me?"

"I am saying, Colonel, that you *lie* about the success of your insane raid on Russia. You never made it over there. You crashed in the desert, and dragged your *guilty ass* back here. To play the hero."

Sturgis controlled his bunched fist and calmly stated, "It's *you* Burns, who is insane. You've been cooped up here too long. Lost your—"

"Gentlemen," the President cut in. "I think we should table all discussion of the mission to Russia and discuss the proposed evacuation. I think Sturgis has a point. If he—"

"Bah," Burns said, and looked at the picture of Florence Nightingale on the far wall. The others, though, including Turner, were willing to listen to the colonel.

Sturgis described the mysterious secret fortress called Fort Collins (see CADS #7) and told how Indians from a reservation near the fort were willing and able to help them. He told them that Robin, his wife, was being treated by Indian doctors, at that reservation. That Robin had been too sick to make the trek to White Sands. "Chief Naktu has many good men," Sturgis finished. "He has braves that we can train to replace our lost technicians. With their help, we can activate Fort Collins. You can't imagine the firepower and supplies in that fortress."

Burns, though he had pretended not to listen, now shouted, "Ah, so that's it! You want to lead us into a trap! The Indians are holding your wife and—"

Van Patten snarled back at the general, "Oh, *shut up!* We've all had enough of you the past few months. I think you should remove yourself from this room, General Burns, if you are planning to be disruptive."

"Only if the President says so," Burns fumed.

Everyone looked to Williamson. He took a long time to say it, but finally diplomatically suggested, "Perhaps we could talk privately later, General. Just us two."

"Ah," Burns smiled, and backed toward the door. "There you have it! The President wants my advice; he appreciates me. He trusts me. Well, there is no reason for me to listen to all this gobbledegook!" He smiled, "Williamson, I'll see you *later.*" He winked and went out the door.

Once their irritant was out of the way, the group quickly agreed with the President that an evacuation was called for. The vote was unanimous, except for Turner. But Turner always went along with a majority. It was Burns who plotted and planned to overturn decisions. Burns would be trouble, Sturgis decided.

But what wasn't trouble these days?

Next on the colonel's agenda was personal business. Very personal: Morgana Pinter.

When he knocked on Morgana's door, she flung it open and the frail beauty clung to him and wept for a long time. She wouldn't let the colonel go. Sturgis, overwhelmed, kissed her and kneaded his hands through her long raven locks until he finally stemmed her tears, and then he pulled away. He went in with her and shut the door, locked it behind them.

"Morgana," Sturgis said, "Some things have—"

"You found her! You found your wife. She is alive."

"Yes," the colonel said, looking down.

"I *knew* it," the fragile beauty said, "I could feel it in you. You felt withdrawn from me."

"Morgana," Sturgis sighed, seating her on her single cot, "It isn't you. It's the fact that she's my wife. I knew her before you, we had years—"

"And I'm just your girlfriend, your *mistress*—is that it? I'm just a roll in the hay, nothing serious." She started to quiver and Sturgis put a blanket over her bare shoulders.

"You said once that you loved me," Morgana whispered.

"I do."

"No, you don't! You lied!" Her eyes widened in anger. "And you lied about other things!" She suddenly lashed out with a stream of words, "You said Pinky wouldn't attack as long as I was here. But he did. He killed most of us, destroyed the base."

"I don't think Pinky did it. It was a Soviet bomber that did the job. You must realize that, Morgana." Sturgis was beginning to wonder if Morgana had also been prey to the paranoia that had afflicted Burns.

49

Paranoia from being underground too long, and from being at constant threat of death.

"Well," the beauty huffed. "The Reds wouldn't have known where this base was, unless Pinky told on us. And you *promised*, Dean. You said I should stay here. That I'd be safe here. That Pinky wouldn't want me dead, and that therefore the base was safe, as long as I stayed here."

"I thought so, Morgana. If I was wrong, you can't know how sorry I am. I've been wrong before, and my mistakes have killed many people. I do the best I can." She had succeeded in making him feel about two inches high. The colonel sat down beside her and buried his head in his hands.

Soon he felt her long, cold, slender fingers caressing him. And she lifted his head and she kissed him, on his closed eyes, on his lips, on his chin. "Dean, oh Dean, forgive me. I don't care about anything now. I want you to make love to me. Just make love to me. Please. This once. Forgive me and make love to me."

It was a cold and brutal world, and her body was warm, and her lips so soft. Thoughts of Robin, of duty, of the pressure of time, faded away. Morgana slipped off her blouse and shucked her silk pants. All was forgotten in the age-old ritual of man and woman embracing in the most intimate way.

When they were dressed again, Sturgis sucked a long drag on a stale Kool cigarette, and, as its menthol cooled his lungs, said, "Morgana, we're evacuating White Sands. Today. We're going to another secure base, near where I left Robin. The President has ordered all personnel to be ready at 0900. Can you pack up that quickly?"

Morgana, who was combing out her long black hair

50

at the mirror and had been humming softly to herself, said, "What's to pack? It's all in the closet in a suitcase. Never unpacked."

"Then," he said, standing up, "I'll see you at the disembarking area." He felt cold and hard and guilty for his indulgence. He really shouldn't have made love to her. But Sturgis had needed it, and maybe she did too. She knew it was all different now. She had accepted the fact that now that Robin was back, she was going to be *nothing*. But she still wanted him.

"Dean?" she whispered his name, like it was a sacred word.

"Yes?"

"You *did* love me, before you knew about Robin being alive."

"Damnit. I still *do* love you. It's just *different*."

"Yes. It's different," Morgana agreed. "But you're still some damned great roll in the sheets, lover boy." She meant more than that, he knew it. She was being — brave.

"Morgana?"

"Yes?" she stopped combing her hair and came close to him. He wished that she had dressed. She looked too damned alluring, too beautiful. He wanted to do it again, but there wasn't time. The colonel found the words he meant to say with difficulty: "You've gotten stronger, Morgana. It's good to see that the stuff Pinky did to you, I mean it's good to see that what he did to you didn't . . ."

"Permanently fuck me up? Permanently scar my mind?" she finished. "Like the scars on my body, the mental scars have mostly faded. Yes, I *know* I've gotten better. Thanks to you and the people here at White Sands. I can stand on my own two feet now. I'll manage without you, too, Dean. I'll be good about it. I won't try to pull you from Robin. I want to meet her, as a matter

51

of fact. I want to be friends with her. Will—will she understand about—us?"

"She's a hell of a woman, Morgana. Like you. She'll understand. Hey, do you have another stale Kool?"

Chapter Eight

Sturgis hated to leave Morgana—but he had to. The President's order was to check out the new C.A.D.S. suits that had been developed in the test cavern over the past several months. The rest of the colonel's men were at the motor pool re-equipping and checking out the new tri-bikes.

Sturgis entered the vast testing cave, a natural cavern, connected to the base through the E level blast door. He saw the young genius Brian Martel turn and look up from a bank of consoles. The electronics whiz was standing there with Van Patten who, as the chief scientist of the base, was responsible for weapons development.

He hadn't noticed it in the business of the hospital room, but now the colonel became aware of how much both men had changed. Oh, Martel, at age twenty-eight, still was a young man, but his curly black hair was dulled, he was much thinner, and there were bags under his eyes. Van Patten had gone the opposite way in his weight, put on maybe twenty-five pounds in all the wrong places, and had gone completely gray. The strain of it all. And being cooped up . . .

"Ah, there you are, Colonel. It's about time," Van Patten criticized, "don't you know we're on a tight schedule, Colonel?" Van Patten didn't wait for a reply. He went back to working at his buttons and dials, leaning over so that his long gray locks fell forward into his face. Sturgis wondered if the hawk-nosed scientist would manage to set fire to his hair with his cherry-red pipe.

Martel came to shake the colonel's hand, "Welcome to the new reduced-and-less-efficient testing range, Dean. Ignore His Highness's testiness today. I think Van Patten is just anxious to show you our latest modifications to the C.A.D.S. suits."

Sturgis nodded, and looked over at the rows of shiny silver suits hung on the left wall, beyond the clear blast-glass. He whistled. "You've sure been busy here. Just how many new suits are there?"

"Twenty. That's all we could manage. But they have the modifications you requested before you left on Mission Russia: More mini-darts, and less powerful but more compact electro-ball shells that are lightened up a bit. That modification alone should make the backpacks lift you easier, use less fuel. Plus of course we kept the VSF function. You can still load almost any Russian-calibrated shells and bullets into the firing system. And now—I hope—there'll be no more jamming. Plus our team has added a few mods of our own."

"Sounds great. Er, what's the special modification you put in on your own?"

Martel grinned broadly. "Oh, you're gonna love this." He looked to Sturgis just like a child about to show off his new toys. "Dr. Van Patten?" Martel asked, "Could you turn on the test area lights now?"

Van Patten didn't turn or acknowledge Martel at all, he just grumbled and pressed buttons at the console. The irritable man lit up the distant part of the natural cavern with floodlights. Then he turned. "If you two are done jabbering, shall we begin?"

"Well," Sturgis asked, "I suppose you want me to fetch one of those suits and get inside, and go out there into the cavern and try it out. Right? If so, you better open up the blast-glass and let me get to it."

"No need for that," Martel smirked, "the suit will come to you!"

"What?"

"Just watch this, Colonel," Martel said, taking the seat next to Van Patten. The whiz-kid of White Sands base flipped a switch and said, as way of explanation, "Dean, the suit on the far right rack is called Zeus. That will be your suit. All the suits are named now, after Greek or Hindu gods of old." Martel put his mouth to the mike and said very clearly and loudly, "Zeus, come here! Zeus, come here."

As the colonel's jaw dropped, the empty suit raised its metallic arms and grabbed hold of the hooks it was hanging on. It lifted itself off the pair of hooks and jumped down the three feet to the cavern floor. It landed awkwardly, and seemed to totter for a second. Then the C.A.D.S. suit stabilized, turned its mirror-bright visor in their direction like it was looking at them, and began striding toward the console. Its walk was like a sort of bridal gait. Or a mummy, perhaps.

"This is some kind of joke isn't it, Martel?" Sturgis asked. "Billy is in that suit, right? You've been putting me on. Very funny; for a moment I thought it was moving of its own accord! — I admit it."

"Zeus," Martel said clearly into the mike, "de-opaque your helmet."

The helmet visor of the suit coming toward them now cleared. Sturgis saw nothing inside the helmet but the back of the helmet!

"Can you beat that," he said, astonished.

Martel bragged, "Something, isn't it? It was inevitable of course that we'd develop a call-system. You

55

know, Colonel, that we had a sort of remote control on the tri-bikes and that we have already experimented with remote for the suits as well."

"Yes, but that was very limited."

"Well it's not limited any more. These new C.A.D.S. suits have artificial intelligence 80396 chips in them. They can even learn, and make suggestions to you! — Zeus, go to the back of the test cavern to area A. Use your Liquid Plastic Fire-mode to demolish the second target on the right."

"It can *fight?*" Sturgis was incredulous.

"Watch."

The empty C.A.D.S. suit now responded to Martel's order. It spun on its heels and staggered off toward the far end of the cave. When it got there, Sturgis watched in awe as it raised its right arm, and from the firing nozzle a hell-fire of flames shot out. The flames engulfed a plastic target, setting it afire in a mini-second.

"That's enough, Zeus," Van Patten said. The chief scientist turned and glared at Martel. "Sonny boy, you know that we can't waste ammo on meaningless demonstrations; you *know* that!"

Martel said, "Oops sorry." He didn't sound very sincere.

"I get the picture," Sturgis cut in, "and I'm not sure I like this modification at all. If the suit can do all of that by itself—"

"You're not replaceable yet, Skip," Martel said, "It's just an edge—an added edge for you and your men. There are circumstances in which you will want to use this new function. For instance, if you're out of your suit and wounded, this mode of op could come in handy. Like Roy Rogers calling Trigger when he's downed by an outlaw. Just call Zeus."

Van Patten laughed. "There's a more likely use for the new function, Sturgis. Your men have gone crazy

56

out there in the field many times. So next time one of your C.A.D.S. supermen *flips his bonnet,* you can call his suit by name, and override his functions. I approved this function so it will be possible to neutralize any of your hotshot nuke-troopers."

"I see." Sturgis took a deep breath. "Can I get inside the damned ghost-suit now and try the firing systems out? I've had enough of the walking-zombie-killer bit."

"Be our guest," Martel said, opening the blast door. "Zeus, come here and dissemble yourself for the colonel. —Call him by his name, and he'll do anything."

Sturgis frowned. "I hope Zeus doesn't decide to do his own thing when I'm inside!"

Once he was in the air-conditioned silence of the new suit, Sturgis took a few tentative servo-assisted steps. He found the walk mechanism smoother than in the old black metal suits. The feel of the new suit was light, very light. That was good. Now to see if the firepower was all right.

At Sturgis's signal, Van Patten pressed a button and the clear-plastic blast shield slid up into the overhead rocks to let Sturgis enter the far part of the test range. "Don't tarry, Sturgis. And don't waste ammo," Van Patten admonished.

"I promise," Sturgis said. Then he loped to the far end of the cavern and began working the systems. The sensor modes all checked out, and then he picked a series of targets. The first target was a moving dummy on a cable. "Prepare smg mode," the colonel said. He pointed his right wrist and turned it a fraction and said "Fire." A set of explosive bullets headed toward and demolished the man-target.

That was okay. "Now for the E-ball . . ." Sturgis cut off Van Patten's shrieks of rage as the scientist realized that lots of ammo was about to be wasted. Sturgis fully checked out all the weapons systems. It only took a few minutes, but the cavern would never look the same again. Practically every natural rock formation was blasted to hell by the advanced weapons systems of the new C.A.D.S. unit, by the time the colonel was satisfied.

When Sturgis headed back toward the console he tried to use the jet-pack on his back. He underestimated how powerful it was—or how much lighter the new suit was. Sturgis banged the helmet against the cavern ceiling! He eased up a bit, and then glided to a two-point landing before Van Patten who seemed to be shouting at him. Of course he couldn't hear, for he still had the external-audio cut off. Sturgis clicked it on, and heard the end:

"—report this outrageous use of materials to the President," Van Patten was saying, red-faced.

"Thank you," Sturgis said, taking off the shiny helmet. "I like the new suit fine. Does it come with two pair of pants?"

Once the colonel was de-suited, Martel walked him back a way into the corridor, and asked a favor, "Colonel, there's one extra C.A.D.S. suit. I can wear that one, can't I?"

"Well," Sturgis said, "I suppose so. We've always tried to leave you at home, keep you under lock and key, because we couldn't afford to lose you, Martel. But now you'd probably be safer out there in the real world in a C.A.D.S. suit than as a civvie . . ."

"Great. You won't regret it."

"I know. Oh, Martel?"

"Yes?"

"Raise your right hand."

The young man did.

"Do you promise to follow orders, eat your Wheaties,

and support and defend the constitution — even the equal rights for women clause?"

"Yessir!" The electronics genius smiled.

"I now make you a sergeant. Obey orders or be court martialed. Kapish?"

"I kapish," Martel said.

Sturgis said, "I'll send the other men around now to be outfitted. Tell them nothing about the Zeus-function. At least don't let Van Patten explain it. They won't like his reasons for having that function in the suits."

"Yessir."

Sturgis patted the young man on the shoulder. "Good work, Martel. I like the suits." The colonel turned and walked away. When he was out of sight of the young man, he walked slower. Sure, he liked the new suits. But they wouldn't be enough. Not really. The Russians had computerized attack-defense suits like these too. By the thousands.

How long would World War Three go on? How many more nukes and germ bombs would fall before mankind called it quits and let the Earth start licking its wounds, the colonel wondered, as he walked. Would the people of this mad planet fight to the last man? Fight until everything was dead?

Maybe. And if they did fight on, until only one man was left — Would the last man stand up and scream out at the sky *"Why?"*

— And, would that man be an American, or a Russian?

And would it matter?

Chapter Nine

Suited up in their shining new battle gear, seated in the new tri-bikes, the C.A.D.S. unit assembled in a V-formation, looking invincible. The men revved up their low-slung three-wheel motorcycles, which were as gleaming new as their nuke-armor suits, ready to move out. Sturgis looked around and waved his hand to the blast-door controller on the platform. The fumes were building up, so he wanted the repaired main south blast doors open now. The huge, half bent door creaked open very slowly on its tortured hinges, and Sturgis beheld the red dawn sun refracting in the dust-devils outside.

"Move 'em out," Sturgis ordered, and he directed his point vehicle forward with a gentle push on the throttle. It felt good to be moving and to be outside. Underground was for moles.

Once the whole unit was three-hundred yards out on the sands, Sturgis ordered a halt. As the dust they had raised died down, he scanned the rest of the evacuation party with his tele-mode. He saw that President Williamson's mobile hospital unit—actually more a war-wagon than an ambulance—was right behind the tri's. He knew Fenton was at the ambulance's wheel, and Nurse Waters was in attendance on the President, who was still on an I.V. The mobile hospital unit looked, the colonel thought, a lot like the Rhino big-wheeler they had once roamed nuked-out America with, dealing the Russians telling blows. But this truck-sized spherical wheeled ambulance was not bristling with gunports. It just had a few anti-air missiles crammed on its roof.

The ambulance had no Red Cross symbol on the side. A Red Cross these days just let the enemy get a better bead on you! This Sturgis had found out by hard experience.

There were thirty other battered old vehicles: half-tracks, old Mac and Mitsubishi trucks, and a few jeeps, behind the twenty-seven C.A.D.S. troopers. A large convoy, three hundred and sixty souls in all, including thirty-one children. They were all that remained of the U.S. Government and its personnel. He sighed. How the hell was he going to make time when half those vehicles would break down soon and need a tow truck to move them in a few hours?

With resolution that he would do the job, the colonel, sounding confident, radioed, "Okay, off we go! Follow my lead, keep in formation unless instructed."

As the roar of the tri-bike and truck engines filled the desert, as the cloud of easily detectable dust and exhaust fumes rose a mile high, they gathered speed. Up to thirty miles per hour. Sturgis didn't want to push that limit. Better to go slow than to be not moving at all.

"Remember, C.A.D.S. troopers," he announced on a select channel, so that only the metal-clad warriors could hear, "we have a bunch of civvies and a lot of rusty half-shot trucks in the convoy. So go easy on the gas. Besides, the tri-bikes are more fuel efficient at thirty. At least we will stay at that speed until we find some fuel."

Martel, who was riding slightly back and to the left of the colonel asked, "How many mpg do these babies

61

go?"

"Ask Jepson, from motor pool," Sturgis said.

From back in the last row of tri's, Jepson piped in, "These new models go about eight miles a gallon at two hundred mph, our top speed. They do twice that at a flat one hundred, six times that well at thirty. That means we are right now getting forty-eight miles per gallon. And we have ten gallon tanks."

"See what I mean, Martel? Jepson is an expert. We have to find fuel—any kind of fuel—within four hundred and eighty miles."

"What's the chance of that?" the young genius asked.

"Pretty good," Tranh, who had studied the problem, radioed. "The gas tanks of the abandoned vehicles on the interstate rust more slowly than the car and truck bodies. The new-mod tri's can take some pretty damned sludgy fuel. They'll even run on alcohol."

"If you see a scotch warehouse," Fenton interjected, "please let me have a wee bit first before you go pouring anything fine into that damned gas tank!" That brought responses like "Amen!" and "good idea!", plus a lot of laughs.

Sturgis heaved a sigh of relief as they got to the Devils Pillar area and spread out. White Sands was now about eight miles behind them. They moved on in silence until Tranh spoke up, "Dean . . . I have a funny feeling."

"What kind of feeling?" Sturgis asked the Vietnamese-American, who was the most intuitive of the bunch. Often Tranh's hunches turned out to be dead-on.

"That we're about to be . . . in trouble."

Sturgis didn't feel anything, but he trusted his second-in-command's instincts. And he acted on Tranh's feeling. "Men, let the civilian vehicles go ahead, move 'em out fast—get the trucks behind those boulders."

"What's up, Skip?" Billy asked."

"Nothing, I hope."

"I feel it too," Fireheels said. "Something's about to happen."

As the colonel watched the trucks get behind the field of granite boulders, he received a radio message from Rossiter, who had the job of maintaining sky-alert: "Skip, there's company up there; something's falling." Soon they all picked the sky-object up on their screens.

"Computer analyze object you are tracking," Sturgis ordered.

Inside his helmet the readout announced in brilliant red, "NUCLEAR TIPPED SOVIET MISSILE, TRAJECTORY TO-WARD WHITE SANDS BASE. ESTIMATED IMPACT TIME, THIRTY SECONDS."

"All tri-bikers — Get behind that boulder field," he ordered. As Sturgis took the rear and headed for cover, he actually saw the black streak in the azure blue sky. A shiny, metallic cylinder. "Shield your eyes, everyone!" he exclaimed as he just made it behind the boulders.

The nuke hit, but there was no explosion.

"A dud?" Rossiter asked, after a stunned moment of silence.

"Maybe," the colonel replied dryly. "I'm going up top to have a look."

But Sturgis had barely gotten off his tri when Fire-heels, who had moved of his own initiative, reached the top of the largest boulder. "Skip," he reported. "I can see the damned warhead lying on the ground near the base doors! It's sort of moving."

"Come down here."

"Can't hear you, Skip."

"Then for God's sake, put your visor on full-power opaque, in case the damned thing—"

"Done. —Skip, something real strange. The war-head is crawling . . . it's digging itself into the ground. My God, it's head is like a drill . . . It stopped throwing

63

up dirt now. I think it reached where it wants to be, and it is about to—"

The flash was as bright as the noonday sun, and the near-instantaneous shock wave sent Joe Fireheels's suit aglow, and sent the Indian flying off his high perch like a burning Phoenix bird.

Chapter Ten

Sturgis watched with great apprehension as Fireheels tumbled away like a leaf in a windstorm, totally out of control. He was about to jet up after the Indian, when he saw the Apache hero use his jet pack to stabilize. Fireheels radioed, "I'm okay, stay where you are, I'm coming in."

Soon the nuke-trooper landed near Sturgis, who saw that Fireheels's suit was still smoking hot from the flash of nuke heat. Joe's signal was static-filled as he smiled through his singed visor and said, "The old model suit wouldn't have taken all that heat, would it?"

"You crazy son-of-a-bitch!" Sturgis replied, slapping a metal hand on the Indian's back. But there was little time for more celebration. The warning signal for another shock wave was reverberating in their ears, and everyone flattened out on the ground.

When, a second later, the shock wave hit, it took the top off centuries-old rock pillars. Of course, it did no damage to the C.A.D.S. men, but Sturgis was worried about the civilians in — or under — the trucks.

A quick check by the armor-suited men, however, confirmed that there were no casualties, and the radiation was low.

Sturgis jetted up to the top of the now smoking

boulders. He scanned in the direction of the base with tele-mode. The visor, automatically compensating for brilliance and radiation, showed a rising black and orange smoke cloud. A mushroom shaped cloud.

Billy alighted next to Sturgis, and then Fireheels was up there again. Billy spoke first. "Can you beat that — a tunneling nuke! Those Reds are pretty clever."

"And deadly," Sturgis reminded, "That nuke was big enough to take out the remaining levels of the base. If we had left a half hour later than we did . . ."

"We'd all be blown to bloody hell," Fenton piped in from the ambulance below. "Shouldn't we push on, Colonel?"

"Yeah." Sturgis said, "We should."

Sturgis kept the convoy together, and they were lucky enough to not have a breakdown. But the weather was changing. The temperature rose precipitously as the day wore on. Overheating problems were inevitable. Overloaded thirty-year-old trucks don't run cool!

Once they were seventy-one miles from the abandoned base, Sturgis saw the rad-count drop to near zero. The winds were favorable, sending the fallout to the west, away from them. Lucky again. They came to several narrow passages between vast tumbles of rock. The famous "rock sculptures" area of Arizona. Except the nearby hits of nuke-warheads during the Soviets' surprise attack had tumbled most of those million-year-old rock formations. It was a messy area, with most roads blocked. But they'd have to get through.

Sturgis asked Fireheels and Billy Dixon to ride to the top of a rise and scan ahead, find them a route. As they did so, the colonel bided his time thinking what a fool he was to attempt a different path back toward Fort Collins. He had reasoned that if his unit had been tracked via Soviet spy-satellite cameras on the way to White Sands, the Reds might land paratroops along that route, expecting that when the Americans found the base "destroyed," they'd return along their old route. But was this detour worth it?

Joe Fireheels reported from the hill, "Skip, there are three narrow ways to get through this badlands. I'll feed the coordinates into the computer-link, so you can have a look."

"Right," Sturgis said. As he sat there on his idling tri-bike, the map-like computer generated holograph was projected before his eyes on his visi-screen. He whistled. "We'll have to divide the convoy into three parts," Sturgis concluded. "The largest vehicles take the middle route—that means you Fenton, and the trucks. Do you copy, Fenton?"

"Bloody right I do! I'll be lucky not to jam this hospital unit between two boulders, Skip. I'll do the best I can."

Everyone else was instructed, and then the convoy split up, each group toward separate passages about thirteen miles apart. As an afterthought, the colonel sent a pair of C.A.D.S. men to lead the truck group. If something should happen—say encountering a Red patrol or some bandit gang—the civvies would need the C.A.D.S. firepower.

But there were no major problems. An hour later, the convoy rejoined, minus two trucks. One had broken an axle, another truck's engine blew. The personnel from those trucks had doubled up in several others. They rode on, as day turned to dusk.

"Hey, Skip," Billy said, "You know what time it is?"

"Yeah. Why? Is your watch broken?"

"Not that kind of time." Billy drawled out. "It's almost time for the Jerry Jeff Jeeters show! That Bible-thumper might have some info for us."

"Yeah," Martel said, "and did I mention I programmed the whole Bible into our suit-computers? If Jeeters starts giving out messages in his Bible-code, we can instantly get a translation."

"Okay," Sturgis said, "Try to pick up his TV signal—channel 89, UHF. Tune it in as we ride. But keep an eye on the terrain too."

Sturgis watched a small square TV screen light up on the side of his helmet. Clear as a bell, the video monitor in the helmets showed the Communist hammer and sickle superimposed over the crucifix. That was the logo of station WSOV in Hartsdale, South Carolina. But the logo stayed on, and strains of Soviet martial music erupted, instead of the preacher appearing.

"Skip," Billy asked, "do you think the Reds have gotten wise to Jeeters?"

"Yeah, they probably found him out, at last," the colonel frowned. "I hope he committed suicide before they tortured him. Remember Jeeters in your prayers."

Finally, the screen changed, and the blasphemous logo faded away, to be replaced by blue letters announcing "SPECIAL BULLETIN." A voice-over announcer said, "Ladies and gentlemen, there has been an important vote in the Supreme Soviet Assembly. Please stand by . . ."

"Vote? That's a laugh," Billy snorted, "We killed the entire Supreme Soviet. (see CADS #7) Besides, they just rubber stamp the Premier. And we killed him too!"

"Shut up Billy," Rossiter snapped, "Let's see what's going on."

The words faded from the screen and a middle-aged man in blue serge with oiled-down hair appeared. He smiled broadly, showing gold molars, and said, "As is custom in completely democratic, peace-loving procedure of Soviet state, the people have spoken through their representatives. They today chose a new Premier, as our glorious present leader has chosen to retire early. Ladies and gentlemen, the new Premier of the Soviet Union will address you now, with simultaneous translation into English. He brings good news for all mankind!"

"This good news I gotta hear," Billy mocked.

The screen faded, and when an image appeared again, it was of a grim man behind a large mahogany desk. He was facing away from the camera, studying a wide window filled with sharks and other fish. The broadcast was from a submarine!

When the man turned, Sturgis almost ran his tribike into a ditch. He gasped, "Oh no! *Veloshnikov* is the Premier!"

Billy and half the others exclaimed as well. ". . . worse than before!"

Yes, it was definitely Veloshnikov, the battle-scarred insane general who had started the whole thing. The man who had masterminded the surprise attack on the U.S. that began World War Three. He was the new Red leader.

Veloshnikov smiled, and started to speak in Russian. His words faded a bit and a woman translator began her work. She said, "I, Marshal Mikael Veloshnikov, Lenin's heir to power, ruler of all the world's territories, conqueror of the nine continents, am pleased to announce that my first act as your leader was to utterly destroy the last vestiges of the rebel illegitimate United States government. Peoples of the world may rejoice, for the so-called secret emergency White House at White Sands, New Mexico has been eliminated. The outlaw gang known as the C.A.D.S. unit or Omega Command has been utterly extinguished."

"Not *quite*," Sturgis muttered.

Veloshnikov turned the page of his prepared speech

and continued, "We wish to commend the American patriot Pinky Ellis for his work in helping the loyal socialist forces detect the White Sands target." The cruel twist of Veloshnikov's lips seemed to break into a warm smile for a second as he added, "Dostevedanya, Americansky dogs."

Then the TV-screen faded back to the hammer-and-sickle logo. The oily-haired announcer appeared and said, "Reverend Jeeters Gospel Hour will no longer be shown at this time. Stay tuned for our new comedy program, 'I LOVE LENIN,' starring—"

"Cut the signal off before we get sick," Sturgis said. "Come on, let's move it! We've got a job to do." He revved up his tri-bike engine and pulled out ahead. "When we get to Fort Collins and get the equipment there operational, we'll see whose country's defeated and whose isn't!"

Chapter Eleven

Sturgis had been depending on his suit-compass and inertial guidance mechanism to plot their position as they travelled. He was much surprised when he took a reading an hour after they passed the tumbled rock area and found out that they were in Cairo, Egypt. Or at least the readout *said* they were in Cairo!

Cursing a storm of blue words, he had Rossiter and Billy confirm his readout with their own equipment. Results the same. A quick run-down on all systems made the C.A.D.S. commander realize that all systems were way off. Some a little, some a lot. The new C.A.D.S. suits' guidance computer couldn't be trusted.

"It could be magnetic interference," Martel said, apologetically. "Extra-strong dissonance in the ionosphere, maybe caused by that nuke hit behind us."

"Never mind the reasons," Sturgis snapped. "Anyone have an idea as what the hell to do now? How do we find our way?"

"Wait till dark," Fenton chimed in, "and take a few star-readings for bearings. Find direction the way ancient man did."

"The sky is cloudy," Sturgis retorted testily, "if you haven't noticed. And those clouds are full of dust, we can't expect a clear view in a patch of sky. Besides *all* guidance systems are screwed up, including the sextant function, remember?"

"How about the old road maps we have?" Billy said. "Find a road or landmark, figure out where to go from there."

"Possible," Sturgis said. "But it's been years since the highway department sent guys out here to fix roads, right? A lot of roads and landmarks have been obliterated. Still that's a good suggestion. Men, next time we cross some tarmac, we travel along that road until we find a rusty route marker. Keep your eyes peeled."

Sturgis frowned as he stared out at the desert's emptiness from his low-slung tri-bike. He ruminated about the dilemma they were in, and blamed himself. Again he had made a mistake. Hadn't he learned never to trust damned machinery and computers? Because of his mistake, the remnant force of Americans now were, to put it in a single word, *lost!*

Fireheels now spoke up. "Don't forget about me, kemo sabe," the Indian stated. "Give me a chance and I'll find the way. Let's just keep going in a straight line, until my instincts show the way. Instincts don't need readouts."

Sturgis acquiesced. If anyone could steer them right, it was the Indian tracker.

So they pushed on, scanning for old roads. When they came over a barren hill, Joe Fireheels asked them to pull up for a while. He opened up his helmet visor and seemed to sniff the air. "West winds smell different," he mumbled. "That wind smells right over there so we go that way," he pointed. "That way is west. And the sky is a little brighter there too. I say that we are south of where we want to be." He sniffed again, and cocked his head to the side. "And there is a road in that direction, Skip. When we reach it, we should turn left."

"How do you know there's a road over there, Fireheels?" Billy scoffed. "Do you smell buffalo chips?"

"Ignorant white-eyes," Fireheels mocked coolly, "you don't know a thing about anything. Macadam paving crumbles, over time. And when it does, it leaves an oily odor on the air."

"Listen to Fireheels, Billy. He's your boss — for now," Sturgis announced. "Everyone, follow Fireheels."

They pulled out again. About three miles farther on, sure enough there was an old two-lane blacktop. It cut diagonally toward some distant hills. They got on the pavement and began to travel along its cracked and weeded surface.

They soon came upon a marker. A pitted, nearly rusted away sign that said "County 45." Fireheels consulted the old map and said, "This road is about twenty miles south of the San Ferano range of mountains. We are only a bit off course. We should continue along it for several miles, and then follow the larger road ahead, which is not on this map."

"How the hell do you know it's there?" Sturgis said, "You really must be some kind of shaman!"

"Not really," Fireheels said, a smile flickering on his lips. "My tele-mode system is functioning again. I scanned ahead, and picked up an Interstate highway."

Sturgis now saw the words, "TELEMODE SYSTEMS RESPONDING," flash in his helmet, and laughed. "You had me there for a second, pal."

Billy said, "Well, I ain't trusting no machines no more!" He opened up his visor and dug his own weathered old Exxon road map out of his utility belt. In a few seconds he exclaimed, "Skip, I found this road. Fireheels is right. We're not far off course. We pick up the main highway up ahead, and that takes us back to Fort Collins. Almost directly."

With a rousing set of cheers, they again got under way. They were able to speed up to fifty mph because the temperature was down to twenty degrees Celsius,

73

and the flat hard surface of the road made it easier for the civilian caravan following to keep up without a breakdown.

"Skip, do you see what I see?" Billy said.

Sturgis, scanning ahead on telemode, now saw an abandoned oil truck. It was apparently undamaged. They increased speed to one-hundred and soon pulled up to it.

"Blue Whale Refinery," the pitted paint on the tank truck's side stated. "Best Crude in Texas."

"Rossiter," Sturgis ordered, "Check out the tank. I hope to God there's a lot of oil in there."

"My scanner says there is," Mickey responded.

"Check it manually," Sturgis snapped. "Enough with these computers."

Grumbling, Rossiter stepped from his tri and clambered up on the tilted tank truck. He opened a valve and peered in. "Can't see, too dark."

Fireheels went over to a nearby stand of small pine trees, cut a switch. He went back to the truck and handed Rossiter the stick. The mechanic probed the tank. When he pulled the stick up, it was covered with a sticky black mass, up about halfway.

Rossiter announced gleefully, "Skip, there's a half tank! About a thousand gallons. It's all pretty heavy with rust and sludge."

"Martel," Sturgis ordered, "can you come up here? Tell us if this oil is too sludgy? You designed the fuel injection on the tri-bikes."

Martel's tri-bike was parked way behind the others, but the trooper had already dismounted and was now approaching. He took a gander at the oil on the stick, took off a glove and felt it. "Heck no," Martel smiled. "With the new modifications to the tri-bikes' fuel units, they can handle anything. And did I mention that all the other vehicles are diesel, and that despite their miserable appearance, they have been fitted with the new fuel systems? They all will run on nearly anything now — thanks to my revolutionary fuel injection nozzles. Not to worry."

The cheering was deafening.

Martel did some exaggerated bows. He then walked around the truck. He was inspecting the tires. "Still some air. Skip, you might want to use the air pressure in these Firestones to pressure an oil recovery tube. Save some of our own air systems."

"Good idea, Martel. I'm sure glad you came along!" Sturgis said. "Well, let's get to it! We have miles to go before we sleep! Fenton, bring up the mobile hospital. You're probably lowest on fuel, I don't want you to stall out."

Fenton, once the tri's made way, pulled the big-wheeled vehicle up alongside the oil truck. "Fill 'er up," he demanded to Billy, who by now had the end of a hissing jerry-rigged pump hose in his hand.

"What am I? Some bloody petrol station attendant?"

"Wipe my windshield, will you please?" Fenton added. "And check the battery."

"This here station is American self-service. You Brits can bloody well take a flying—"

"Sticks and nukes will break my bones—" Fenton jested, "but names will bloody well never harm me!"

Sturgis had to smile. Not because the jokes were good, but because all the personnel were now cheery. At least a lot cheerier than you could expect, seeing that they were the last of the American government, and way out in the wilderness searching for a new home. The colonel had to admit that he, too, was in good spirits. Veloshnikov was sure they were all dead. But not yet! A line of Mark Twain's came to Sturgis. Twain told an audience that had believed rumors that he was dead, "The reports of my death have been greatly exaggerated." Well, America's death, also, had been "greatly" exaggerated—by Veloshnikov!

Once all the tri's and civilian vehicles were refueled, Sturgis and Tranh conferred. With Billy and Fireheels looking on, they went over the map and took some readings. The colonel decided that they could leave the road and take a shortcut toward Fort Collins. Going through high country would save some precious time, Sturgis concluded.

Tranh was the single dissenter. He said, "Four point seven klicks! That's all we save." There was a hint of worry in his sibilant tones. "Not enough to make it worthwhile."

"Every little bit helps," Sturgis replied, whistling as he got on his refueled tri. "Move 'em out!" He led the column out toward the east. Later the colonel would regret not paying more attention to Tranh in the giddy moment of optimism. That casual decision to take the high ground would turn out to be one decision he would rue for a long time!

They were on a sloping rise, and down to twenty klicks per hour, when Rossiter said, "Skip, my unit's Blue Mode is at optimum, and I'm getting a reading. It says there's a group of six men, about one and one half miles ahead."

"Armaments?" Sturgis asked. He cursed. Even on manual override, shutting down all other systems, he couldn't get the Blue Mode up on his fancy new Zeus-suit.

"Negative, Skip."

"Confirmed," Billy said. "Six unarmed hostiles. They'll be at visual range in—five minutes."

Sturgis thought for a second, then said, "We pull over, and wait. So they can't hear our engines."

Soon Sturgis was able to use tele-mode to see the people approaching. And they didn't look dangerous. Quite the contrary. A pathetic lot. A man about thirty years old, flabby at the belly, encrusted with dirt from his beard to his toes. He carried a club with a rock jammed into its forked open end, and his slack jaw drooled a stream of saliva. A woman full of breast and belly, like she was several months pregnant, equally filthy, with tangles of long hair half braided, followed the caveman. She had a gaping wound on her cheek, still red with blood. And the rest were kids.

"What the hell are those, Skip?" Billy asked. "Are they people? They're walking sorta like apes; you know, knuckles to the ground. And they're nearly naked."

"Billy, it's a family of Americans. Just starving, naked Americans. We've seen their like before."

"Like that?" Martel half groaned. "What's wrong with them? Are they becoming animals? Has it come to this?" The young Edison was apparently greatly upset.

Sturgis realized how Martel felt. After all, the electronics whiz hadn't spent much time out of White Sands base the past few years. Sturgis replied, "Worse than that, Brian. You don't know what we've seen out there in post-war America. The worst and best in what we call the human race has come out since the war. Some people are de-evolving."

Sturgis could clearly make out now that the cave family carried bows and arrows as well as the single club.

"Can't we help them," Martel asked. "We have some extra food, and some matches, and a few rifles we can give them to hunt."

Sturgis sighed. He didn't want to delay, but after all, Martel was right. After all they were still human beings. "Okay — a ten minute stop for basic humanitarian aid, Martel. That's all," Sturgis said.

Chapter Twelve

The "cave-people" family, when they saw the tri-bikes coming, were alarmed. They started to bolt and then as the nuke-troopers gained on them, the bearded man grabbed the woman's arm and shouted out something. They stopped in their tracks and turned to face the approaching troopers. Sturgis figured the man had told her it was hopeless to run. It was common sense that made the six of them just stop in their tracks and watch them coming. There was nowhere to run, nowhere to hide. They couldn't outrun high-tech equipment like Sturgis rode.

As Sturgis and the other troopers bore down on them, the two adults of the family stood more erect and they saluted. Of course! They had stopped running because Sturgis had an American flag flapping on the antenna of his tri!

The husband and wife, with the children hiding shyly behind them, watched as Sturgis pulled up and stepped from his vehicle. He took off his helmet and said, "Don't worry, we mean you no harm. We want to help you. We represent the President and the U.S. government." Sturgis noticed now that they weren't totally naked. The family wore tight-fitting tattered skins of some sort. Skins as dirty as their own. Not much protection against the building west wind, or the coming night.

"Oh, thank God," the woman said, and came forward and fell at the colonel's feet and kissed his metal boots. Sturgis quickly pulled her up and said, "Billy, break out a few fatigues for these people. Give them some water and rations. Get some kids clothes from the civvies."

Soon Billy had handed each of the family a tear-open plastic bag of K-rations. "Eat that," he said, "it has all the vitamins and stuff you need."

"Well," the caveman said, staring at the unappetizing looking bar of K-ration, "actually, we're not hungry."

"You're not hungry?" Billy was amazed.

The woman looked disconcerted for a second. Then she said, "We get by. My name is Martha Carswell. This is my husband."

Mr. Carswell said, "Maybe the kids want some. It's okay, Martha, feed the young 'uns. We could use a little water, if you please."

The little sandy-haired girl took a few nibbles of the K-ration she was handed, then spat it out. "Ugly-bad," she protested. "Why can't we have our regular food? This stuff stinks!"

"Shhhh," The husband scolded, hushing her. "Soon enough, Betty. Soon enough, we'll eat right. Drink the water."

Once the pathetic family was dressed in normal clothes and had a few sips of water — Sturgis didn't let them drink more than a sip or they might get cramps. The parch-lipped man told his story of survival: "My name is Carswell, Alan Carswell. Me and my wife and kids were originally from Salt Lake City. We were on a camping trip to Yellowstone Park when the nukes hit, those long years ago. At first, we managed pretty well, considering. That was the first few years. Keeping to remote areas, finding canned food, shelter. Folks weren't as crazy back then. We had to go to more and more remote areas since then, to avoid the disease and madness. We ran out of supplies and if it wasn't for running into the Saloonkeeper and his group, we would have died. But the Saloonkeeper's bunch don't have much, not the past month. We volunteered to go out and try and bag a few small animals. And to check the small traps we rigged out here. We get a prairie dog now and then. We had one a few miles back. Had to eat it ourselves, so we could go on hunting. That's why we're not that hungry."

"I see . . . Who's the Saloonkeeper?" Sturgis asked, rubbing the hair of the smallest blond boy, who was chewing on a Baby Ruth candy bar that Billy had scrounged up from supplies. Evidently that candy was a hit, unlike the K-rations.

"Saloonkeeper is a real nice man. He runs our small town." The man picked up the boy and wiped his face. The kid was not very experienced with candy bars. He was getting chocolate on his over-long sleeves of his uniform shirt, and around his mouth.

Morgana now drove up in a jeep, obviously curious as to what was going on. Morgana jumped out of the jeep, came forward, and bent down, just to make conversation with the little girl, who looked angry or about to cry. Morgana asked, "What kind of skins are you wearing under that new jacket of yours? It looks like pig skin."

"Yes," Alan Carswell interjected, suddenly strangely nervous. "It is pigskin. We—we used to have a few hogs," he continued, "until the disease hit 'em. Like I was saying, things have been getting harder and harder."

"I don't see any other life forms on the readouts, Skip," Billy said. "Hunting must be awful around here."

Mr. Carswell nodded when he heard the remark and

80

said, "Well, can you beat that! Your equipment can tell you where there's animals? Hell, we could sure use some high tech equipment, back in town. The Saloon-keeper will be pleased we found you men. He'll be happy at that, though we didn't get any game. Yessir, he'll be happy that we're not coming back empty handed."

"I'm not sure we can stop in your town," Sturgis said. "Where is it?"

"Not far. You've gotta come," the woman pleaded. "There's no canned food, no medicine. Surely you can spare a little." She looked back at the caravan of trucks and the big mobile medical unit that now were moving up along the slope of the mountain. "My God, that's quite a convoy you have!"

"Please come, help us out," the husband pleaded. "Lately our town has been raided time and again by an old National Guard unit gone renegade. It's run by this black bastard Sergeant Renquist. A real killer. Renquist's people got real nasty on the last raid. Killing and stealing women."

"Stealing women?" Billy asked.

"Yes," the woman looked down at her toes, and muttered, "They — one of them renegade guardsmen — took my oldest daughter Christine. Just took her. We never saw her again."

"After that raid," the husband said, "we set up guards, armed ourselves best we could. But we ran out of ammo and now we don't even have bullets for hunting."

"Enough," Sturgis said. "Sounds like a bad situation. But we've got to be on our way. We have a mission. — Rossiter, find these people a few hundred rounds and a half dozen M-16's." He turned back toward Mr. Carswell. "That firepower should help," Sturgis smiled. He started to put his helmet back on.

"You can't leave us!" the wife said, "Please come see the Saloonkeeper. He can tell you what we need most!"

Sturgis sighed, but he demurred. "The war is still on, miss. We've got to go on."

The husband asked, "Please, just a short way. The Jerrards, and the Hogans—families that joined us a few months ago—they're sick."

"Yeah," the wife agreed, "they're all real sick. Their hair fell out after they ate the canned asparagus they found out in the desert."

"Radiation," Morgana whispered. "Oh no."

"Yeah, maybe," the man said. "But now they cough like pneumonia. Their hair fell out, but it's growing back. They're thin and cough now for weeks. Spit some blood too."

"Any red spots?" Sturgis asked, dry-mouthed. He had seen the nuke-spawned Red Death disease once, and that was once too often. It was incurable. And highly contagious. (See CADS #1)

"No spots," the man said, "I'm sure it's tuberculosis."

"Simple antibiotic will clear that up," Morgana said, her dark eyes pleading to Sturgis. "We can have the nurse check the sick at the town, and then we just drop off medicine. We have enough antibiotics for a few months."

Sturgis shrugged his shoulders, and said, "Okay. Where is this town?"

"Just over that ridge," Mr. Carswell said happily.

"Get on the backs of our bikes," he told the family members.

They quickly complied. The kids were excited by the prospect of a motorcycle ride. And Sturgis found that the sullen kids could actually laugh.

The town looked a lot like a movie set to the colonel,

and he mentioned that fact to Alan Carswell, who rode on his tri-bike.

"It is a western movie set," Carswell replied. "We finished building ten of the best set-houses. Until the guardsmen came, nobody came here. We have a well that still works."

"Where is everybody?" the colonel asked, as they rode down the main street. He saw a sheriff's office, a church, a clapboard general store, and some hitching posts.

"They're probably in the saloon. The building with the black flag on top of it."

"Why a black flag?"

"It's our town flag. Hadda have something."

Sturgis eyed the black flag with suspicion. "Carswell, why not the American flag?"

"We had one. But the raiders stole it," the man explained.

"What's that big whitewashed building a hundred yard past the town?"

"Oh that? That's the Supreme Veal Company Building. It was an old factory farm. Here even before the movie company! That's where we got the black flag. The flag says Supreme Veal on it. Saloonkeeper says we hadda have something in the American flag's place, temporary like."

Sturgis's questions were interrupted when the radio crackled. Tranh's voice came up on it. "I don't like how this feels, Skip," the Vietnamese said.

"Suggestions?"

"None. Other than dumping this family in the main street here and leaving."

Sturgis nixed the suggestion, thinking it was a remark very unlike Tranh. They rolled on down the empty streets of the movie set town. "I've learned to trust your instincts, Tranh. But we won't stay long," the colonel said. "What can anyone do to us anyway in our outfits? — Visors down, gang. Keep sealed, just in case."

Thus feeling safe in the deadly metal cocoon of hellfire, the colonel rode down the main street.

"Pull 'em over right there," Mr. Carswell said, "Pull the bikes up in the diagonal spots in front of the pharmacy."

As they did so, a group of well-proportioned people, some wearing better versions of the pigskin clothes of the Carswell family, with added bone jewelry, came out of the pharmacy.

The C.A.D.S. men all dismounted. Fenton came out of the armored ambulance-wagon and also strode along with Sturgis. A top-hatted man — the mayor? — approached. The Brit had left the door of the ambulance open so the President could see.

Sturgis was expecting no challenge, at least none that could even dent a sealed C.A.D.S. suit! But suddenly a pair of telephone company "cherry-pickers," the kind of equipment they once used to fix overhead wires, came springing up from behind the pharmacy. Before any of the C.A.D.S. troopers could realize what was happening, high pressure water hoses poured out yellow lines of liquid from the top of the phone-repair towers. Hoses manned by laughing townies who stood at the top of the extension-towers.

"What the hell," Sturgis wondered aloud, "Why water?" The colonel half laughed, "Well, water won't affect us!" He raised his hand, to fire a warning shot. But he heard a sharp grinding noise. And then his hand froze half way up.

"Glue!" the colonel exclaimed. "They're firing glue-streams at us. Fire at them, everyone. Smg fire! Get those men on the towers!"

But no one could raise an arm — literally. And then there was smoke coming from his C.A.D.S. suit-mechanisms. Sturgis, and probably all the other men, had to shut down their servo-motion circuits. Or they would overload and fry in their immobilized suits.

"Now," Carswell said, striding over to the man in the top hat, "we have them."

"Take these metal men inside," the mayor said. "We open 'em up like canned caviar."

"I want the fat one," a skin clad, bone-necklaced tubby woman in the pharmacy crowd laughed. She waved her nail-ended club in the general direction of Van Patten, who was standing, frozen in fear, just beyond the immobilized troopers. Van Patten had drawn a gun, but it had been knocked out of his hand by a gang of ragged tykes. There were a few shots from the civvies. But the situation was hopeless without the C.A.D.S. firepower. There were thousands of the townies, heavily armed with all sorts of pistols and rifles, even a few flamethrowers. Once a few civvies fell dead, it was all over.

Sturgis couldn't even move the helmet, but when the fat woman came into view he recognized that the club she was carrying wasn't a stick. He realized that the club was a human femur. A human leg bone! And as he watched, the woman and some of her toothy drooling friends gathered about Van Patten and poked at his plumpness. Then the colonel understood what these people were.

Cannibals! These people were cannibals!

Chapter Thirteen

The helpless C.A.D.S. troopers and the civilians of White Sands were trapped, and Sturgis knew it. The bone-necklaced savages that had once been ordinary Americans now whooped and shouted in glee as they went about their work. Each C.A.D.S. man was being lifted and carried away by three or four of the muscular men into the pharmacy. Like statues into a museum. The civilians were herded into a tight group, poked and even bitten to see how they would taste.

But the struggle was not quite over! There was the sound of sudden gunfire. And several cannibals fell in a hail of bullets coming from the parked trucks. Sturgis was in a position in his immobilized C.A.D.S. unit where he could see the source of that withering fire — on his left. He shouted out encouragement on his ampli-mode, which still functioned.

President Williamson had managed to crawl out of his ambulance bed and crawl to one of the machine guns mounted on the war-wagon/ambulance. He had been overlooked it seemed, in the general roundup. And that oversight was costing the cannibals plenty! The hero-president wisely confined his fire to the area of the C.A.D.S. men, knowing that way, stray bullets would not kill those on his own side! What moxie

Williamson had!

However, the big .40 caliber weapon soon ran out of shells. And while Williamson fumbled to reload the Browning, the bastards rushed him. They easily overpowered Williamson, ripping the trailing I.V. line from his arm, and carried the swooning man over their heads into the pharmacy. Sturgis figured the President had cut down about thirty of the savages. And he was not surprised when the little ragamuffins running about started sucking and biting on the fallen townies among them.

Sturgis was afraid the crowd would start dismembering the President at once, they were so angry. So he did the only thing that came to mind. He told the cannibals who they had captured. Maybe there was shred of Americanism even in these human-flesh eaters: "Stop," Sturgis shouted out on his half-conked-out, sputtering ampli-mode, "that is the President of the United States you are carrying there! For God's sake—"

The flabby-faced man with the top hat stuck his jutting jaw close to the colonel's visor and shouted, "And I'm Genghis Khan! So what? Food's food!" He laughed, sticking his fishy tongue onto the visor and sliding it over the plastiglass. "You look a little stringy in there, soldier, but when we boil you up and add some spice, you'll be good enough for stew. As for this President of yours, he looks more tender. He'll taste real good with a little barbecue sauce."

"Cannibal asshole!" Sturgis exclaimed, "you don't seem to understand. We're still at war with the Reds, we need the President. You—"

The man's fat face moved away from the colonel's view and Sturgis felt his suit being repositioned horizontally. Sturgis realized that he was being carried into the building.

After that, Sturgis was facing a wall filled with

posters of "Gone With The Wind." So he saw nothing, just felt the blows on his suit and the heat of various devices the cannibals used in a futile attempt to peel the C.A.D.S. armor off him. The colonel heard screaming for a while, like some of his people were being skinned alive. That was probably exactly what was happening!

Even after an hour or so had passed, the frustrated cannibals were still unable to remove the leader of the Omega force from his suit. They had turned Sturgis around during the application of a heavy power drill and an electric saw, both of which blew themselves out on his armor. The colonel saw that the half dozen other troopers in the room also were still intact. Immobilized, but intact.

But time had done for the cannibals what their stubborn application of violent means couldn't. Sturgis could hardly breathe any more. The suit was bereft of oxygen supply. He reluctantly recited his verbal open-sesame code, the proper sequence of numbers to get the suit open. All the C.A.D.S. men were dying of suffocation because their air exchanges had been sealed by the streams of glue.

When he felt his helmet bolts rise up, Sturgis heard the gleeful noises of the cannibals, felt their hands twist his helmet off. Sturgis looked around. He had to admire his men. Only now were they too succumbing to the inevitable and opening up their suits.

Sturgis didn't have much time to look around, though. A meaty fist slammed him in the jaw and he saw stars. "Getting stuffy in there, was it?" The same fat-faced man in the top hat sneered and hit Sturgis again.

Sturgis stared with unabashed hatred at his tormentor, vowing to himself that it wasn't over yet. The troopers would probably be tortured now, he realized. Tortured to tell how to operate the suits. It was a tough thing to contemplate, but maybe there would be a chance during the torture session, to trick their captors.

The woman the C.A.D.S. trooper had "rescued" — Mrs. Carswell — now came up, still wearing her fatigues borrowed from the U.S. government convoy. "Well, looka your face, all runny with blood," she sneered. "You who was gonna give us a few lousy guns and some terrible food and push on! Well, this armor suit and all that equipment is gonna please Saloonkeeper no end. Not to mention all the food you people will provide us. We'll smoke-cure some of you and save you for sandwiches."

"Sandwiches, sandwiches," several of the other cannibals took up the chant, dancing around the de-helmeted C.A.D.S. men and laughing.

"You're all disgusting." Sturgis shouted, "You should see yourselves as I do!" Then he had an idea, so he shouted out, "The Saloonkeeper would be ashamed of you all. You're not smart! He would have better use for us!"

They stopped dancing around and looked at one another. Fat-face finally said, "Maybe the Saloonkeeper is done with his siesta now. Maybe we should take these guys down to him and see what he says."

Sturgis's demands to know what happened to the President — and the other civvies — went unanswered. All the C.A.D.S. men were shorn of their frozen-up suits quickly, now that they had unsealed their statisbolts. Sturgis was tied up so that he could barely hop! They were then manhandled out the pharmacy door and led down the dusty street toward the "Mars Saloon."

Sturgis was shoved through the swinging double doors. And once his head cleared from the dozen blows that had been delivered on the way, he saw a typical movie-set type of western saloon. Complete with naked-lady picture behind the long bar. Complete with "cowboys" gambling at the round green-felt-covered tables. Complete with a man behind the counter, a bartender in white shirt and red sleeve-garters wiping up the counter.

The barkeeper looked up when the captives were hustled forward and he smiled. His long face reminded Sturgis a bit of the old-time actor John Carradine—one of the colonel's favorites. But this man had a peculiar lifelessness in his cold green eyes, and there was something perverse and slovenly about how he held his wet lips.

The top-hatted creep kicked Sturgis in the groin with a spurred boot, and as the colonel doubled over, fatface shoved him to the floor. "Bow to our leader," the roughneck insisted. The crowd of captors managed to get every C.A.D.S. man to his knees by kicking him in the shins or groin, and shoving. The man behind the bar just watched and kept wiping the counter. He received a brief rundown of the capture of the C.A.D.S. unit and civilians from Mr. Top Hat.

"Who's the leader," the barkeep finally asked.

The jowly man pointed the colonel out. "His name is Sturgis."

"Ah, I thought so. Those eyes have leadership in them. I'm the Saloonkeeper. I run things around here. What do you think of our town?"

"Fuck you, whoever you are, bartender," Sturgis said, peering at the man through a haze of red.

The long-faced man smiled, and he ducked under a space in the counter and walked up to Sturgis. He peered down and said, "Now, you know, I don't like being called bartender. I'm the Saloonkeeper. Remember that. I'm here because I want to be here, which is more than I can say for you! It's just something I like to do, tend bar."

"And eat people!" Sturgis snarled. "We are representatives of the U.S. government. We demand you release us or suffer the consequences. If you harm a hair on the President's head—"

"Testy fellow, aren't you," Saloonkeeper said, staring down without blinking at the colonel. "Well, I like that. So I'll tell you a little about myself. My name used to be Benny. But I'm known as the Saloonkeeper in these parts. A name many have come to fear. And respect. I am the leader because I provide for my flock. Times are hard. Most people are starving out there." He swung his hand ninety degrees, horizontally. "All over the U.S. they're starving and sick. But not here. Not in Supreme Veal Town!"

"You're a cannibal. That makes you a non-person," Sturgis said. "You're a savage, filthy animal."

For that remark Sturgis received several more kicks, until the Saloonkeeper called a halt to his tormentors. "So I'm a cannibal," the Saloonkeeper said, "At least I and my fellow citizens are alive. Cannibalism has its detractors, I'm aware of that. But survival is the name of the game now."

"Do you realize who you're dealing with?" Sturgis asked, trying again to change the situation. "We are *American* forces, on a mission, an important mission, against the Reds. You're an American. Don't you want to defeat the Reds?"

"Ah, the Reds! Yes, we ate several Soviets the other day. They're very dry! At least the ones we found in the desert were dry and stringy." The Saloonkeeper laughed and the crowd followed with raucous laughter. Then the Saloonkeeper asked, "Tarlick, are they all out of their combat-armor?"

"Yes, your highness," the fat-face replied. "This is the

lot of them that had the weird suits on!"

Saloonkeeper grabbed Sturgis under the chin and forced his face up. "So you don't like Reds? Well, we don't like *anyone*. Still, we'd like all of you loyal Americans to stay for dinner!"

Sturgis said, "That will only fill your bellies. We can give you supplies; you don't have to eat people. Look, I can imagine what you've all been through to come to this. I'm not making a moral judgment. (Actually Sturgis was planning to burn these people to ashes first chance he got, as there was a Federal Emergency law calling for the immediate execution of all cannibals.) But we can do a lot more for you than provide a few meals."

"Well, I know that!" The Saloonkeeper said, "But we already have those supplies that you offer, and the glue covered armor suits will be cleaned and made operative. You will show us how to operate them! Believe me, we have developed many ways to make the most reluctant man eager to spill his guts. And then we will have you all as meat on the table! We will be the most powerful group in the nation with your equipment, never short of food again. Right men?"

There were cheers all around. Except from the captives, who cursed and insulted the Saloonkeeper.

When the uproar died down, the Saloonkeeper added, "By the way, that man you said was the President does look a bit like Vice President Williamson. I've had him kept alive, until we discuss things further. Though I don't know why you'd call a vice-president a president!"

Sturgis exhaled in relief, and said, "He is Williamson. Arthur Williamson was the vice-president. But Armstrong died, and now Williamson is the President! Look, we can still win this war the Reds started. We —"

At that point, the Saloonkeeper burst into a loud

92

horselaugh. *"Win?"* He laughed long and hard again. "My dear fellow, who cares any more? The planet is finished. I've not seen a living corn stalk or carrot or bean plant for three years. And we've looked far and wide! No deer for two years. Once we finish eating all the people we can find, there's nothing left to eat. But thanks to your equipment, we'll all be old and gray before we run out of people to eat."

"You *can* raise crops, Saloonkeeper. We can give you seeds."

"Too hard! Eating what's in handy supply — people — will do for years to come. We need meat, not veggies."

"And you'll even eat the President?"

"Most assuredly, I will, sir! I shall call it my 'Presidential dinner.' I shall bring out the finest silver and plates. You know, I have had much less in life. The war has been a boon to me! You see, I am an actor. I did a lot of summer stock. I was fortunately on location here when the nuke-war happened. I played in many Shakespeare productions, but at the time of the bombings, I was reduced to a bit role in a bad western. But now, I'm top bill! You may recognize some of the others here from the movies as well. Many of us are actors. And actors eat when and where they can! But no more scrounging meals at lunch counters. Now we are in charge!"

"Listen," Sturgis said, shaking cobwebs from his battered head, "we'll forgive all that happened so far, and take you with us to a new home. A home that has every luxury. Provided you treat us right, we can lead you to an Eden."

"Promises, promises." The Saloonkeeper rolled his eyes ceilingward. "I kinda like it here. I kinda like the taste of human flesh. Especially the ones we create into human veal."

"Human veal?" Sturgis, knowing from experience

that it's a lot harder to kill someone you've had a long conversation with, kept the conversation going.

"Ah yes, we keep the best of our captives alive in 'veal crates.' You know how veal is made, don't you? You crate a young calf, and you don't let him even move more than a foot for years and years. You force-feed him lots of milk and nutrients, and he gets anemic and fat and soft. Then he — or she — is very tender and tasty. We have already had success adapting this process from animals to humans. At the Supreme Veal building."

"That's about the sickest thing I ever heard."

"Really? Thank you! Well, it was done to animals all the time before the war. People like the taste of veal, and they don't care if a bit of prolonged torture goes into the making. Now there is no veal calf, but we still have human veal. We will use the children you have brought us, raise them chained up in the veal crates. You adults, you've already grown too muscular. Oh, I don't suppose you can understand our love of human flesh, Sturgis. Hmmmm. Maybe a little demonstration . . ." The Saloonkeeper snapped his finger, "Martha! Bring the snack you've prepared!"

The woman Sturgis had encountered earlier came out of a doorway and placed a silver tray with a cover on the shiny surface of the bar. The Saloonkeeper ordered Sturgis shoved along as the cannibal leader went to the silver tray and lifted its cover.

Sturgis saw a piece of meat covered with onions. No, it was a human hand. A man's flabby hand, with a ring on its index finger that he recognized. That was Van Patten's engineering school ring!

The Saloonkeeper took a fork and used it to break off a finger. "See how easily it breaks? With just a fork, you can cut it. Here —" He held the finger on the fork up to Sturgis's face. "Try it!"

"Bastard! Animal!" Sturgis said between clenched

teeth, and turned his head.

"No? Ah well, more's the pity! You'll be sorry you didn't have this snack, let me tell you that!" The Saloonkeeper sucked on the finger and once his teeth had cleaned off the bone of all its meat, he swallowed.

"You may take it away, Martha. — Men, put this captive with the fat ones in the first big stew! I tire of his comments. And do what I said about the children, make sure they're all sent to the veal crates. Keep the President on life-support for now."

"How's about the girls, boss? Can we have some fun first?" The fat-faced man spoke up.

"Oh I suppose so, Tarlick. But that reminds me. Put that dark haired pale beauty, the one called Morgana, in my bedroom. Dress her properly. You know, like a dance-hall madam."

Sturgis realized that Morgana was again to be a captor of a mad butcher. This time someone, some *thing* worse than Pinky Ellis! What mad destiny kept placing her in that role? But at least she wasn't to be cooked, like he was about to be!

America's brightest and bravest, America's future leaders, were about to be lost down a bunch of cannibals' distended stomachs!

Chapter Fourteen

Sturgis was spared being part of that night's stew only because the Saloonkeeper made a last minute decision. He laughingly said he would conduct an experiment. It would prolong the colonel's agony. Saloonkeeper ordered that two adults, as well as the children, be placed in the veal crates. Sturgis and Billy Dixon, because they were the loudest complainers of the captors.

Billy and the colonel had to be trussed up hand and foot with even more rope after they managed a furious struggle with just the slight movements possible in their bindings. Sturgis was pleased that he managed to crack a few ribs and knock a few teeth out. He was pummeled to a fare-thee-well for these efforts, however. And then the two of them were manhandled away to the Supreme Veal Building.

Once inside the building, Sturgis's ears were assailed by the wails of dozens of children. He couldn't see them, they were all packed away in the refrigerator-sized wooden crates placed here and there across the sawdust-floored expanse. Then the colonel was given a blow to the head that put him out cold.

When Sturgis awoke from the blow, he found himself in a different situation. Gone were the seeming miles of binding rope. Instead, he was standing, or rather slumping, in a box. He was chained in place, naked, by his ankles and wrists. He almost moaned and then instead, applied every inch of muscle he had to attempting to tear out the chains from the wood. They didn't even move! Evidently the crate was steel-reinforced. What now?

There were spaces in the slats of the crudely made veal box, so he could breathe. And he again heard wails and cries of the doomed. Children's voices.

He peered through the crack that was at about eye level. In the one large crate in the rows next to him, was someone too large to be a child. And Sturgis saw a shock of platinum blond hair sticking an inch above the open topped crate. It was Billy, chained as Sturgis, rigidly in place by legs and arms.

"Billy," Sturgis whispered, so he could scarcely be heard above the crying. No response. The other nuke-trooper was still out cold. Sturgis, by moving his head to the extremes in each direction — about six inches — surveyed the rest of the grim scene around him as best he could. The colonel saw through the crack that there were rows and rows of crates in the veal shed. The cream of America's children, to be kept in a box for years, softened, made fatter and more tender, for the palate of cannibals!

"You'll pay . . ." Sturgis muttered, thinking of the Saloonkeeper. The low, moan-like wailing was the most sorrowful sound Sturgis had ever heard. It rended his soul to hear it. This was a fate worse than death for sure, for him as well as the kids. And when he thought of that, Sturgis couldn't help feeling sorry for all the calves that had been similarly kept in crates for years. He was sorry for every bite of veal he'd ever eaten. It was one thing to slaughter an animal, another to do this. He never had thought about it much before. All the millions of veal-calves in warehouses all over America before the nuke-war. Animals immobilized, force-fed for years and then freed only to face the grill. That was too much.

The children! His eyes grew red at the thought of them growing up for three or four years chained in the crates, their only attention being when they were force-fed. Their excrement hosed out from the crates by high-pressure water hoses. How many times a day would he be force-fed? Eight, ten times a day? Until he was a blubbery pale thing, that's for sure.

No! Don't think like this, he told himself, don't give in to despair. There was a way out, there *had to be!* He would never give in to despair. *Never!*

A half hour or so passed, and Sturgis tried every few minutes to rouse his companion. No response. Then the big door creaked open, letting in the cool of the desert night — the veal house was kept quite warm. It was, of course, the feeder. The large hirsute man in levis and dungaree jacket came in pushing a wagon of some sort. The "slop wagon," Sturgis would bet. The wailing was punctuated by words of, "I want my mummy!" or "Please, please . . ." All the pleas fell on calloused ears.

"What are ya all wailing about, eh?" The feeder shouted out. "You're gonna be fed," he snickered. "More than anyone has ever been! Fed till you little rascals are plump and juicy! Not many people in this old world will eat like you kids!" He snickered, as he turned in Sturgis's direction. "I can see you lookin' at me, shitface! You two experiments there are gonna like *your* lunch. I'm the guy you broke the ribs on, Sturgis, and so I mixed your meals up myself. I threw a bit of extras in for you two! And I'm gonna like giving you two some extra goodies over the years." Laughing, the feeder came over and hit a resounding blow on the colonel's captivity box with a hammer. The noise made Sturgis's head spin.

Then the feeder went away with his creaky cart. He was a creature of long habit, the colonel supposed. Probably the feeder always started the feeding at the end of the crate line. The end in the opposite direction from Billy, who was last in the line-up of hell.

Sturgis saw the denim-clad man shove a plastic tube from the wagon up through the crate's slits, and then press a button. Instantly a milky liquid came rushing up the clear plastic tube and into the crate. Sturgis heard gurgling noises. And so it went, until the feeder involved himself in the feeding of the immobilized girl-child in the crate immediately to the colonel's left. He could see her rather clearly, a brunette pigtailed child of about eight. She hadn't been crying much.

Sturgis didn't remember seeing her in the civvie convoy. Perhaps her silence, and the dull staring blue eyes, and her very pale rotund sagging appearance meant the girl was a captive from a much earlier time.

The tube went in the mouth and then a cord over the head, so the tube wouldn't pull loose. Then the pump went on. The girl grew a little fatter. The feeder felt her a bit and smiled, "Today's your day, Samantha. The big day of your freedom!" The feeding didn't stop until the food mixture was coming out Samantha's nose, a white creamy vitamin-smelling, calorie-rich mixture.

The feeder saw Sturgis's attention was on the process, and smiled a toothy grim. "You know, Sturgis, I used to do this in the Ames factory farm out in Idaho. 'Course, there we just used calves. They were much less interesting company. You know, sometimes I sneak a little action into my work with the young 'uns. Get my drift? This job has its benefits!"

"Bastard," Sturgis hissed. "Have you no human compassion?"

Suddenly Sturgis's condemnation was joined by another male voice. Billy apparently had awakened. Sturgis turned his head and saw the crate next to him tremble. The southerner's powerful try at freeing himself from the chains. Then Billy shouted, "We're not animals."

The feeder laughed as he de-coupled the blank-eyed fat girl from the feeder, and as he wheeled his feeder cart up to Sturgis, he said, "The way I see it, it's eat or get eaten. Veal calves made a lot more noises than humans do at first, you know. But after a while, the kids will get just like the calves did. Real quiet. Just shit and eat. They say the mind shifts away from reality after a few months in crates like this. You should see the blank-eyed expressions of the older crate-meat!"

Sturgis's eyes moved to the feeder-man's neck. The shed was dimly lit, but Sturgis thought the man wore a necklace of something that looked like shrunken skulls.

The feeder noticed his stare and smiled, "Aw, you like it? These are infant skulls. The boss, he don't know how to make shrunken heads yet. We use baby skulls, only they don't hold up so well. They're kinda soft, you know. The Saloonkeeper once said he'd give a million to whoever could show him how to make real shrunken heads!"

Sturgis seized the initiative. Greed. Yes, play to the man's greed! "I know how," Sturgis said, "let me out, and I'll tell you how to do it. Then—"

"Not on your life, buster! You're dangerous." The feeder felt the side of his jacket and winced. "You broke my rib! Besides, I can make you tell me how to shrink heads without letting you go!"

The feeder stopped fiddling with the plastic tubes and went over to the side of the shed. Sturgis had to strain to the farthest left possible to peer out and he saw the flaming fireplace. So that's how they kept the shed so warm! He saw the feeder-man remove a poker from the flames, and turn and approach his crate with it. His cold eyes were soon up against the crate's slit, staring maniacally into the colonel's eyes-of-hate. "Now," the feeder said, "if I was to stick this poker into the crate, put it where it hurts the most—"

"I'd still never tell," Sturgis whispered impassioned, "you'd have to kill me, and then you'd get in trouble."

The man lifted the red hot end of the poker so that Sturgis could see it, and then he wavered. Sturgis hadn't even blinked. "You soldiers have training . . . you just might resist too much. If I damaged the veal . . . the Saloonkeeper wouldn't like it."

"Then we have a deal . . . If you have the shrunken head formula, the boss will forgive you for letting one man get away. And reward you for the formula. How about it! You don't want to work in here forever," Sturgis reasoned, "do you?"

"I don't know . . . I think you're too important a prisoner to free . . ."

"I'll sweeten the deal. Let Billy Dixon out; he's just a regular soldier. Let him go and I'll tell you the formula."

"Well . . . yeah, that might be okay. I used to be a blond kid myself once, 'fore my hair fell out . . ."

"Let Billy go, and once I see him make it over the hill, I'll tell you about how to make the skulls of regular-sized men shrink."

"Don't do it," Billy shouted, "don't give him anything, Colonel! Don't make this bastard rich!"

Sturgis was gleeful at the interruption. Billy's carefully timed protest stopped the feeder's dull ruminations. If the southerner hadn't interrupted, the feeder might have come up with "You tell me how to shrink heads or I'll torture the kids." But Billy's protests had convinced the dull-minded feeder that he was on to something, that he should do it! The man wanted a million—a million what, Sturgis didn't know. What good was money anyway? Maybe it was a million gold pieces. Whatever the reward was, the man wanted to be rich badly!

The feeder said, "You won't stop me from being rich!" And he started to fumble through his keys. In a short while, he had Billy's crate open, and he carefully unleashed the Southerner after that. He released one of Billy's arms and then handed him the keys to do the rest himself. The feeder stood back holding a pump-action shotgun on Billy while the man extracted himself from his chains. The naked southerner asked for, but didn't get, the man's denim jacket to wear.

"What now?" Billy asked.

"You jest get outta here," the man said. "Head for the hills over there." He motioned with his head without letting go of the shotgun. He looked plenty nervous, and Sturgis was afraid he'd decide to shoot the southerner.

"Go, Billy," the colonel whispered, and winked quickly. "Once I see you're on that hill, I'll tell him the formula."

The southerner, mumbling about "not liking the feeder getting rich," took a deep breath and then headed out in a trot, and faded into the night darkness away from the town. Sturgis soon saw his silhouette on the hill, as the first rays of a rising moon lit up the sky.

"He's gone. Okay, now tell me."

Sturgis made something up, a long process of adding herbs to milk and stirring and so on that would take days. Even if he knew how to shrink heads, he wouldn't have told. He shuddered to think what would happen if the feeder believed he was lying.

"Well, I dunno," the man said. Sturgis believed the man was beginning to think he had made a big mistake in letting Billy go. "You'd better have told me the truth.

Otherwise—" he held up the poker, which had cooled, but could of course be heated again.

Without another word, the feeder-man seemed to go back on mental automatic pilot. He shoved the plastic tube down the colonel's throat, tied it in place and pumped him full of goo. So much goo that Sturgis could puke.—And then he left the building, muttering the list of things Sturgis had said would be needed to shrink heads.

Ten minutes later, as Sturgis prayed earnestly that Billy would find a way to lose himself out there, and come back and free him, the feeder came back. He was cackling about how he had informed the others of an escape, and they had sent out a patrol to recapture the veal-on-the-loose! "Hyuuuu! Hyuuh! I tricked you, I did I did," he boasted.

"Cheater," Sturgis snarled, "Bastard! Have you no honor?"

Sturgis was counting on Dixon like he had a dozen times in the past. The colonel had realized that the feeder would report the southerner had escaped. But the southerner had lots of smarts; he was limitlessly resourceful. Billy had survived years of hard combat, years of adversity. He had skills at hiding too. They all had a slim chance as long as Billy was free. He just might figure out a way to save them.

A day passed, then two. The feeder, each time he'd come in and do his dirty work—which was five times a day—would occasionally ask Sturgis for clarifications on the process of shrinking skulls. And Sturgis was more and more pressed to explain how the process took a long time, and had to be done just right. He didn't mention Dixon, and neither did the feeder-man.

Sturgis took the lack of gloating over Billy's recapture

as a signal that the southerner hadn't been recaptured. The hours, the minutes, the seconds went by and they seemed endless.

Sturgis would have thrown up, many times. But there was some sort of ingredient in the food-mixture that prevented that. And the third day — or night — he looked down and saw he was developing a paunch!

On the fourth day, the colonel caught himself thinking, "Why hope?" The words had just come of their own accord into his mind, despite himself. And a few hours later a black despair overwhelmed him. The thought of despair rose and rose so that he could hear nothing else. It said to him, "I'll be here until I'm just a mass of protein and fat for their plates! I'll just get weaker and mindless, and be somebody's veal parmesan sandwich!"

The only hope Sturgis had now was to be killed, so that the agony wouldn't be prolonged. He stopped praying for Billy and started to pray that the feeder would soon realize he'd been hoodwinked and use the hot poker too much on Sturgis, to the point that he would die! Die by quick torture, and be spared the lingering torture of the veal crate!

Chapter Fifteen

After an interminable time, during which Sturgis had done all he could do to maintain a state of semiconsciousness, the door of the veal shed burst open. The colonel looked up dully, and pushing cobwebs from his mind, concentrated on the scene before him. He saw that the skin-clad townies were dragging another adult in.

"Replacement for your friend who escaped," smirked the feeder. The brutes shoved their near naked captive forward, so she pitched over on the sawdust with a thud. It was Morgana, bound hand and foot, covered with scratches. Sturgis cried out to her, and her eyes met his over the ten-foot distance. "Dean? Is—that you? We thought you were dead!"

The cannibals seemed amused and let them speak. Morgana, flopping about, trying to get up, managed to get to her knees. "He—the Saloonkeeper—kept me for his chattel. He used me, for sex. And he did something to me, Dean. Something that even Pinky never did. And I had the opportunity, so I hurt him. Then he said I was too rebellious, that he didn't want me any more. That he needed a replacement for his experiment in making veal from adults. Me."

"Enough," snarled the feeder. He lifted her to her feet

by her raven hair and shoved her into Billy's open crate. Sturgis raged and shouted as they chained her in place. She was crying, but the crying turned into a gurgle as the feeder shoved a feed-tube in her mouth and taped it in place. "Saloonkeeper says she's way too thin, that we should fatten her up real fast." More mad laughter as the gang of perverts left the shed and locked it.

Sturgis raged and tore at his iron bindings to no avail. And then, exhausted, he slumped over and his head lolled to the side. He slept with his eyes open, unseeing. Utterly exhausted with the exhaustion of the hopeless.

Billy Dixon hurt. Bad. He had sprained his ankle the last time he had avoided one of the cannibal's jeep-patrols that had crisscrossed the desert for days searching for him. Searching in vain. It wasn't for nothing, the southerner thought, that he'd studied the art of escape and evasion back in boot camp those long years ago. And the years of being with the colonel in one difficult spot after another had honed his skills to a fine edge.

He hadn't been able to get far from the town before Billy had heard the roar of the jeeps. The cannibals evidently hadn't mastered the complex tri-bikes. And they didn't find him. The first time, they passed just inches from his hiding place. Billy had found a hollow desert reed and buried himself inside a dune, breathing through the tube for hours as the jeeps whizzed overhead. Finally, around dawn, they went away, searching miles farther from the town.

The desert had been his friend—and enemy—since that night. Billy had a bad case of exposure and sunburn now, and the last of the water from the mudhole he had found had been used up. He discarded his turtle shell-makeshift canteen. Too heavy.

Billy Dixon headed north, following the stars at night, guessing direction in the day. He'd overheard talk among the cannibals that their enemy, this Sergeant Renquist and his gang of marauders, were to the north. And any enemy of the cannibals was a potential friend of Billy's. Now, in the cold, windy sunset-light, he staggered up to the beginning of an endless chain of rolling hills. His clothing of tied branches and reeds would not be enough tonight, would not shield his nakedness from the cold wind. He had to find food and warmth. A fire would be heaven.

In his fevered, exhausted state, death seemed a welcome friend now. Oh, yes, he thought, I would gladly die, if it was just myself at stake. Yes, Billy Dixon thought, I would gladly succumb to nature and let my bleached bones be picked at by the vultures that were following along above for the past several hours.

But he willed himself to push on, to stumble through the dark. For the others. For his colonel . . . The stars came out in their chilly glory, and there was one particularly red, particularly bright star on the horizon. Mars? No, it was bigger, brighter. A campfire!

He headed toward that light in the far distance, praying it wasn't a hallucination. Of course, it could be just the fire of a cannibal patrol. He could be walking into the hands of those he sought to avoid these past days. But instinct told him that wasn't so. If there was a God in heaven, it had to be the fire of someone who would help.

Billy peered over a sandy rise and he saw the fire — a real big campfire. And arranged around it were some khaki-clad men. Incredibly, they were gardening! They were poking the ground with hoes. And he saw a whole row of something green. Corn! My God, it was corn. There were other men in uniform, carrying MAC-

11's, patrolling the perimeter, just at the edge of the fields of corn, on guard. One two-man patrol was walking away from the very spot that Billy lay flat on. He was lucky, they had just passed where he now lay. Had Billy been here a minute earlier . . .

There was little doubt about the identity of these men when Billy saw the truck with the U.S. insignia on it, parked half behind the fire from his vantage point. Billy could make out that it was a National Guard truck. Probably this was Renquist's outfit. The so-called "evil" black soldier that had allegedly stolen the Carswell's daughter Christine.

Were the soldiers below really just another bunch of self-serving renegades? Or were they true Americans? Billy had no way of knowing.

And then he heard a piece of fabric slap in the sudden rise of wind. And he saw the American flag atop a faintly visible tent. The red, white, and blue colors were caught in the flare of light from the camp-fire fanned by the wind. The American flag was waving proud and free in the wind.

If they bothered to fly the flag, Billy reasoned, there was a chance they still bore some sort of loyalty to America! Or was the flag a cover? A trick like the "ragged family" that the cannibals used just to draw in fresh human meat?

Someone shouted. Words like "Soups on." Billy saw several of the "farmers" put down their hoes and head for the fire. And now he circled the camp thirty degrees, so he could see what was going on behind the fire.

There was a spit—a construction of metal pipe—upon which a long shape was being turned. A large animal—or a human corpse—was on that spit. He smelled meat, and was revolted by the saliva that coursed through his mouth. Was it human flesh he smelled? He crawled closer. Ten yards, twenty. His outfit was just a pile of leaves and reeds. They didn't notice. And once he was a lot closer, Billy looked again. No doubt about it, it was a deer on that spit, not a human being.

And they had some jackrabbits hung up to age near the tent that flew the flag. The southerner decided he had to take a chance. After all, he was weak, and hungry. There was a pain in his gut that was not hunger. It probably meant some infection. He was half frozen to death as well. He couldn't go on any farther.

He briefly pondered sneaking around later and stealing some food and water. But he didn't have a chance of getting down there and back fast. He was too weak. What choice was there other than to stand up and walk down and announce himself?

Billy hesitated. He overheard the men talking, bragging about how soon they would "kill more of those cannibals." That did it. Billy stood up.

"Hey, fellows," he said in his friendliest tone. "Don't shoot. I'm a friend. One man alone. I'm coming over to the fire, hands raised."

Several of the khaki-clad men stood up and trained rifles at him, the rest just kept their place. "Come on in, stranger, we got you covered!" As Billy walked down toward the campfire, one soldier smiled, "Ain't you a sight! Been out there in the desert a while, I suppose? Fred, go get the Sarge. Seems like we got us a cannibal spy."

"No," Billy exclaimed, "I escaped from the cannibal town. I was in one of their veal cages!" Billy explained rapidly, as he walked forward, arms over his head. He felt ashamed to be clad only in the leaf girdle, but it seemed that was what saved him. He just looked too funny, the man said, to shoot. Billy collapsed at the soldier's feet. That was it. He couldn't move another inch, even when he was nudged with a boot.

They fed him, gave him water, and put Billy near the fire, covered him with a blanket. A short time later he was able to sit and drink some soup. Billy was sitting very near the warm fire, and feeling much better when he saw the "Sarge" approach. Renquist was a tall ebony-skinned noble-looking man in a crisply clean fatigue uniform. There were four stars on his epaulets. Renquist said, "Remove that blanket, stranger, let me see what they were all laughing about."

Billy frowned but he did as asked. And Renquist threw his gleaming black features back and laughed long and hard. Then he controlled himself and told Billy to put the blanket back on. "Sorry, mister," the sergeant said, more seriously. "But something funny is hard to come by nowadays."

Billy nodded. "That I understand." The southerner noted the man wore two pearl-handled revolvers as side arms, revolvers set in western style embossed and jeweled leather holsters. "I was afraid you were cannibals," Billy explained, as he sat and drank coffee with the Sarge.

"Cannibals?" Renquist laughed, "Hell, we're just a bunch of weekend soldiers. I'm a basketball player. Or was. We were re-upped into the National Guard during the emergency. After the nukes destroyed most army and air force bases. The Reds missed us "unimportant" National Guard camps, you know. We were set to fight the Russkies, only all the fighting was way east of here. So we decided to stay put and help the local folk, when supplies got short and things made a turn for the worse in these parts. Roving gangs, and such. We did what we could to keep order. Then the cannibal clan moved into that old movie-set town over there." He pointed south. "We hardly got the guns to fight 'em off when they come looking for meat. But we found some ammo

110

in a cave recently, and we're gonna go in and mess with 'em again, and free some of your fellow captives. Steal some of them cannibals' trucks and so on. — Say," the black man ended, "now, what's your story, fella? You say you were captured. Okay. Who else was captured by them bastards?"

Billy explained in greater detail and spoke about the C.A.D.S. unit, and how they had been taken. And the situation with the children and Sturgis in the veal crates.

The sergeant stared into the fire until Billy finished, and then took the last slug of his java. "Hell," Renquist smirked, "That's some story! And the cannibals have all the C.A.D.S high-tech equipment now? Well, that's real bad news for us. Those cannibals are gonna come calling soon and kill and eat us all."

"Not," Billy said, "if you take the offensive."

"What do you suggest?"

"First, could I have some clothes? I'm sick of going around like Tarzan of the desert. And I find it hard to talk strategy half-naked!"

Billy, on the sergeant's order, received a uniform outfit and put it on. Then he stood up and looked hard into Renquist's eyes. "I say we hit the people-eaters before they hit you. That equipment they stole from our convoy ain't easy to use. It takes getting used to. How about it. I know the layout, where the Saloon-keeper lives, where they keep their ammo and so on. I wasn't just being shoved around down there. I kept my eyes and ears open."

Renquist shook his head. "I don't know. If we go in now, it can't be no small raid." The black man continued, "It has to be an all-out attack."

Billy and Renquist were walking now toward the big tent, with several officers of Renquist's group walking along with them. "Too risky," said the man who was apparently second in command. "I say we move out of these parts tonight. Let someone else deal with the cannibals. Save our own asses."

"Let's get inside the tent and look at some maps and hear more from this man," Renquist said, "before we decide."

Inside the tent, Bill was surprised to see a teenage girl sitting down and knitting. The comely blonde looked up and said, "Oh, a visitor? Hi, my name's Christine." She stood up and put her arms around the black leader and kissed him. Renquist gave her a peck and turned and looked at Billy. "From your accent, I say you're a southerner. What do you think of me having a white girlfriend?"

Billy remained deadpan, feeling that he was being put on the spot. Tested. Finally he said, "The cannibals said the girl was taken by force . . ."

"Ha," Christine said, "I escaped from that hellhole! They've all gone crazy, even my folks. They *crave* human meat. And I didn't want to be one of them!" A tear formed in one blue eye. "Daddy said we had to be that way, eat people, 'cause there wasn't enough food, but I don't want to—" She held on to the sergeants massive body for security. "I'm seventeen. I do what I want."

"What do you think of her being my woman?" Renquist repeated, demanding a response.

Billy shrugged. "If Christine is here of her own will, I have no objection."

Renquist smiled and said, "Well, now that that's clear, sit down and we'll discuss this attack you think we should pull."

The other officers were called to join them, and it was soon obvious to Billy that to a man they were not happy to hear about the new situation. They wanted to leave the area, rather than attack the movie-set town. Still, they all looked to Renquist to make the decision.

The second in command, the red-headed Irish-looking corporal Munson, was the strongest naysayer. "We can't take them on," he kept saying. "They have all them new guns and stuff. I say we get away tonight. Now."

But the black man disagreed, "Listen, Munson, it's true that the cannibals now have all sorts of equipment. And lots of ammo. But there's no getting away for us now. They will follow us in their new vehicles—these super-motorcycles Billy here described. The Saloonkeeper won't let us get far, if we chicken out and run."

"What if," Munson said slyly, "this Billy here is some sort of liar, someone sent by the Saloonkeeper to lure us in?"

The black sergeant looked hard at Billy. "I think this young man is telling the truth. If he is, then we'd better launch an attack, before the cannibals hit us. And don't forget—we'll be rescuing the President of the United States, Munson. It's our goddamned duty."

Munson cynically retorted, "Our only duty is to ourselves now." He stared at Renquist a long time. And finally blinked. Munson said weakly, "Well, just voicing my opinion. The men won't like it. They were ready to attack the cannibals until this Billy Dixon here spilled about all that new armament we'll be facing. Now they'll be scared to go in. But you're the boss." He looked down at the blanket he was sitting on. "I just don't like the idea."

There was a long silence.

"Now or never," Billy said. He turned toward the sergeant, and said, "It's up to you."

"I have made the decision," Renquist announced. "We will prepare a big raid, for tomorrow. Advise your troops, Munson." Everyone saluted, and the officers left the tent. Billy and the black man and Christine sat alone and had some more coffee, poring over the maps and lists of men and their specialties.

113

Billy was dismayed. Renquist had a few jeeps, a few machine guns, and about a hundred men. Hardly enough. But maybe, if they kept the element of surprise . . . they could do it.

Chapter Sixteen

Renquist's commandos, under Billy's direction, moved into the cannibals' town unobserved, like a dawn breeze. Dealing silently with the town perimeter's two guards, the raiders were just suddenly *there*.

The commandos split up into three groups. Billy's detachment headed for the veal shed. Soon his contingent of forty commandos, their faces painted with grease, flattened up against the shed's outside wall. Just as the yawning feeder rolled his cart of pasty force-feed food to the door. Billy watched as the feeder opened the padlock. The chump never even looked up. If he had, he would have seen a young platinum blond man just fifteen feet away, seen the man with bloodlust in his eyes. Once the padlock was opened, Billy, with great gusto, slit the feeder's fat turkey-throat.

The commandos rushed inside and Dixon went immediately to Sturgis's crate and started fiddling with the lock, using the keys he had taken from the feeder. The colonel, who had been slumped over suspended in his chains, now looked up, dull-eyed.

"Billy!" Sturgis exclaimed joyfully, "you made it!"

"Shhhh," Billy said. "Not quite yet, Skip. Right now, we have the advantage, but it won't last."

The southerner gave up on the lock, and whispered,

"Jensen! Bring the cutters!" The soldier handed Billy a pair of jaws-of-death four feet long, and Billy used it to snap the lock and then cut open the colonel's chains. Similar work was going on all around the shed. Crate after crate was emptied of the captives. A few of the freed children, roused from their stupor, began to make noise. They were difficult to quiet down, and it was obvious that the rescue operation would soon be detected.

Sturgis, after accepting a khaki outfit, and putting it on, took the cutters. Fighting off weakness and nausea, he staggered over to Morgana's crate and began work. Soon he had extricated the swooned Morgana from her bindings. She, like the colonel, was quickly dressed in out-sized khaki clothing. The colonel roused her with a kiss, and she focused on him and smiled. "Free . . ." she mumbled. Poor frail Morgana bore the marks of many beatings, so covered with weals that Sturgis had to spend a few precious seconds holding and soothing her.

The colonel wasn't in much better shape. The feeder had been taking out his wrath on them both for the past few days. Sturgis's legs felt like numb lead, but he forced himself into action. Turning the sagging Morgana over to a medic of the raiders' unit, Sturgis conferred with Billy and quickly was filled in about the plan of action.

"Over there," said Billy, peering with the colonel out a cracked dirty windowpane, "we have fifty more guys. They're going for the ammo dump. We don't have much firepower—want to steal some more before we hit the saloon. Most of the cannibals are in there, near as we can tell. This squad is to hit the pharmacy, where they keep the C.A.D.S. suits. Maybe we can get one or two operative. We brought along some powerful solvents, to use on the glue messing up the suits."

"Good," Sturgis mumbled, "very good! With even one suit's firepower, we'll win."

"Over there," Dixon pointed, "by the saloon, you can see the third squad—twenty-five men led by the black guy. That's Renquist. They're to wait until our unit and unit two join them before going into the saloon."

Sturgis, peering out into the dust-blown street, saw no townies, just the group of raiders moving on a run, getting into position.

Billy now turned to face the squad, who had made a hole in the rear wall and were finishing the evacuation of the children through it. The southerner announced, "Okay, you know what Renquist said, I'm turning over command of this unit to Colonel Sturgis. He will be in charge from now on."

Sturgis tried to look as 'in-charge' as he could as he surveyed the bunch. The commandos were all kind of skinny, and a few looked like they really didn't want to be here. Probably shitting in their pants, as it was. But they had seen what could be done with proper leadership. They had made it this far, right under the noses of the cannibals. And they were now reinforced with a moral outrage, upon seeing the kids in bondage. The young soldiers were scared, sure. But that showed they had a bit of common sense. They'd do!

"Men," Sturgis said, "There's gonna be a fire-fight real soon. Hopefully we will have more and better weapons by then. But whatever we have to fight with, there's one thing that will make us win. We have right on our side. Now, let's go. Billy, I'm sure, has described what even one of our high-tech weapons can do. If I can get just one C.A.D.S. suit operative, we'll show the bastards what real Americans can do."

They saluted smartly, smiling and nodding. Evidently they all liked the sound of his confident words. "Now," the colonel ordered, "let's go *do it*—the C.A.D.S. suits are in the red-doored pharmacy to the left of the ammo-supply building. We move out through the hole you made, make a dash one at a time across the main street. Everyone waits along the south wall of the pharmacy, until I tell the next move."

They managed a silent and rapid deployment, and the colonel peered into the pharmacy through a side window. There they were, the gleaming C.A.D.S. suits, hung up on a jury-rigged rack along the opposite wall. And there were no guards he could see. Together with Billy and the others, Sturgis went around the back way and used cutters to cut open a metal panel on the door, then reached in and undid the lock. They poured inside, ready for anything. But there was no one.

Sturgis quickly inspected the suits. And he whispered to the southerner, "They've made no progress in freeing these things up!" He took the bottle of solvent from Billy, found some rags and poured out some liquid for both of them. They worked on just one suit, the colonel's. Sturgis had decided that one would do. No time to get them all operating.

In five minutes they had managed to get the mobility joints and the weapons system unglued. Sturgis bolted himself in, as the commandos watched in awe. He tested the circuits, and the readout lit up: "SYSTEMS GO."

"Okay, now we're in business," the colonel said, his voice tinny through the still half-fouled helmet speaker. He turned and selected a group of the shakiest soldiers, and announced, "You six, stay here, guard the rest of these suits. We'll be back." They saluted, glad to have the flunkie-job.

The colonel said he alone would be the right flank of the attack on the saloon, and the rest of the squad, under Billy, would take the left flank. They synchronized watches with the readout-time in the battle suit and then Sturgis had them move out to join the first squad.

As the colonel headed off alone across the dust-blown street, avoiding collisions with a half dozen tumbleweeds, he turned up his detection systems. And he heard piano music and laughter ahead. There was a goddamned party going on in that saloon. God, had they been carrying on all night? If so, they'd be pie-eyed drunk, and tired. That would be a break! Sturgis smiled. The party would soon be over!

The metal clad avenger got closer and closer, savoring the moment. He heard some complaining voices in there as well as laughter. Male voices.

"Computer, analyze voices and give I.D.s."

"Working . . ." the readout announced. "COMPLETED. Male voices, number: three. I.D.: Michael Rossiter, C.A.D.S. trooper, Fenton MacLeish, C.A.D.S. trooper, President Arthur James Williamson, President of the—"

"End sequence," Sturgis said. His heart was pounding wildly. *They were still alive!* He'd have to be very careful whom he shot.

The colonel peered through a knothole in the wall near the front swinging doors and saw the Saloonkeeper. The madman was spinning a roulette wheel, and saying, "Place your bets, place your bets. The winner gets the charming lady on the right as his or her prize!"

Sturgis managed to get a look over to the right. There sitting up on the counter naked and trussed up, weeping, was Darlene, a fifteen-year-old from the White Sands convoy. The bastard was spinning for her. Also over to the right, their hands tied above them to hooks up on the wall behind the bar, were the men of his squad. Rossiter, Fenton. Fireheels. And the President and several others. They had numbers tied to ropes about their necks. At first the colonel couldn't figure out the meaning of the numbers: 235, 198, 177. Then he understood. Weight! They too were being gambled for. Their worth was judged by their weight—their food value!

119

The colonel glanced at the time on the readout. Ten seconds until he was to burst in the front, while the rest of the men hit the rear. Nine, eight . . . He decided to jump the gun, in order to be there when the soldiers got in, and warn them not to fire over toward the bar.

Sturgis creaked over toward the swinging doors of the saloon, and, feeling like Jesse James, pushed them open.

Chapter Seventeen

Sturgis burst into the saloon by kicking open the swinging doors with a big metal boot. The doors tore off their hinges and sailed twenty feet. The occupants turned from their preoccupation with the spinning roulette wheel and dove for cover, their smiles erased. Sturgis, still feeling like Jesse James, fired at anyone who moved too slowly to reach cover. He sprayed bullets from hip-level, like the cowboy gunfighter.

Twelve or thirteen of the cannibal bunch — including Mr. Top Hat — fell spurting blood. A few returned fire from their weapons, but, of course, the bullets bounced off the C.A.D.S. suit. Sturgis shouted out on amplimode — "Okay men, come in now, but avoid the bar area — there's hostages there." A second after he said this, the squad of soldiers led by Billy and Renquist smashed down the rear doors. They were a little trigger happy and nearly hit a few of the trussed-up hostages. Another ten cannibals and a few of the soldiers fell. Sturgis was striding around now using radar-mode to detect the enemy who had hidden behind gambling tables or potted palms. And the colonel riddled those areas as well with his explosive bullets.

"Saloonkeeper? You still alive?" Sturgis called out. "Come out now with your hands up and we won't shoot you down. You and anyone else who surrenders will have a trial first."

In response to the colonel's offer, two of the cannibal bunch, a pair dressed all in black with six shooters held in both hands like a pair of Black Barts, bounded out of a corner and jumped over the bar. The pair knew what they were doing—they put their guns directly on the hostages who hung helplessly on the hooks behind the bar. "Shoot at us and we'll plug your buddies," one of the gunmen snarled. "Now back out of this here saloon real slow, and make sure those jeeps stay back there so's we can get away. We'll take a few of this meat-on-the-hook with us, so you don't get smart, Sturgis."

No way was the colonel going to tolerate letting this pair go! Sturgis had to be very exact and very fast. But that was his business. As the tense standoff went on he programmed in instructions into his suit computer: "Track heartbeats of non-C.A.D.S. personnel quadrant four, and fire at them when clear of other targets." He just held his firing tube arm up, and as one of the gunmen shifted slightly, so that for a mini-second there was an opportunity, the computer announced, "FIRING SEQUENCE EXECUTED." As those words came across the colonel's readout, the two men were expertly blasted by a pair of single bullets, right through their tickers. They slumped over without getting off a shot.

Sturgis cried out, "Anybody else thinks they're wise guys?" There were no takers. "Okay," the colonel ordered, "now throw out your weapons." A scattering of revolvers, UZI's and .45 automatics skittered across the floor from a dozen hiding places.

Sturgis smiled. "Squad, move around and round up the bastards—You men nearest the bar, untie our friends—and get some clothes on that teenager!" Renquist's soldiers complied.

The black leader of the colonel's allies, getting directions from their two-gun leader, soon had the situation in hand, all enemies routed and tied. Billy was mad for revenge. He kept rushing around dragging a hand, a foot, a head, out from behind some statue or overturned table, checking to see if he had Saloonkeeper. But the Saloonkeeper was nowhere to be found.

There was a noise—the creak of a door. Rossiter, who had just been ungagged, shouted out, "Skip—there's a little trap door behind this counter! I saw the Saloonkeeper duck down it!"

Cursing a blue streak, the colonel spun around and crashed back out into the dust-blown street. He scanned up and down, running through the modes until the sound sensor detected a discreet rapid heartbeat a hundred yards down the drag, toward the stable.

Sturgis hit the servo-assists hard, and they heated up dangerously, still being half-clogged with glue. He raced after the target at thirty miles per hour. And soon he caught a glimpse of the fleeing Saloonkeeper on I.R. Mode. Sturgis fired a burst of 9 mm bullets right through some piles of construction material—boards and pipes. The pile exploded into fragments and Sturgis thought he had gotten his man, but the heartbeat appeared again on the readout. And it was somewhere above the colonel! The bastard had climbed up into the hayloft.

Pushing aside frenzied horses, the colonel made his way as quickly as possible through the stable until the readout said he was directly under the enemy. The detector-mode said that the Saloonkeeper had one Enfield .30 cal. rifle. No danger to a C.A.D.S. suit unless it had explosive charge bullets in it.

Sturgis was about to fire a burst through the ceiling and end the life of the miscreant, when he had an idea. Shooting was too good for Saloonkeeper. Way too easy. Instead, he called out, "Saloonkeeper, I'm here, and you're a dead man unless—"

Bullets whizzed by the colonel from the loft above, fired through a crack. And instant analysis by the computer showed that it was indeed a pair of armor-piercing rounds. "Shit! Now what?" the colonel muttered to himself as he pressed against a wall.

He heard running feet above and then a thud behind the stable. The bastard was making a run for it. Maybe he thought he had gotten him!

Sturgis, breathing a sigh of relief, smashed through the plank wall at the rear of the stable. He saw the running figure, and smiled. Yes, he knew what to do now. "Fire mini-dart-grapple," the colonel said, aiming at the man's left shoulder.

Instantly there was a *whump* sound, and the uncoiling steel cable and its stick-in head leapt toward the running man. When it hit, Saloonkeeper fell, dropping his rifle. He gave out an animal-like yowl of pain. The grapple-hook, imbedded in his flesh, was in deep, not likely to come loose. Not that the bastard didn't try to pull it out!

Sturgis, laughing madly, slowly pulled the man in, dragging him back across the dust like a fish he had just caught. A real prize-winning catch!

As the victorious soldiers gathered around, the colonel lifted his catch up onto its feet and held Saloonkeeper by the collar, stared into his eyes. "Well, this is one fish story with a happy ending," he said. "This one didn't get away. Billy—tie this creep up over by the saloon—on that support pole. Tie up the others the same way."

"Why not just burn him to death with my fire-mode?" Billy asked, "I can get my suit cleaned up and then burn him, to make sure the LPF is working."

"No," Sturgis said. "Let's savor this a little."

There was a party atmosphere at the two-minute-long

trials of the cannibals and their king in the town square. The freed captives and the soldiers were drunk and fired off their guns as the captives—one by one—were brought before the duly elected 'judge'. The judge was Billy Dixon. So naturally, all the townies were condemned to hanging.

Many of the lynch-party participants had donned western outfit, complete with chaps and sidearms that they had found in the town prop-building. It really looked like a scene from Judge Roy Bean's old west, circa 1870, the colonel noted with amusement.

Sturgis had saved the best for last. As the other cannibals—men and women alike—were hauled away screaming and were hung from every available place they could be hung, he called for the Saloonkeeper to be pushed up on the makeshift platform.

The Saloonkeeper's eyes were fixed upon one of the hangees who was still gurgling out noises and kicking his life away not far off. "Hey, hey . . . you-you can't do this to me!" the Saloonkeeper shouted. "I'm a citizen! I got rights!"

Sturgis took Billy's seat and just stared at his torturer. He just sat a long time in the sun in the wicker chair they called the "judging chair."

"You have no rights," Sturgis smirked. "Turnabout is fair play."

"I appeal to your humanity," the Saloonkeeper said, getting down on his hands and knees as many of those previously judged had done. "Colonel, don't hang me. Have a heart."

"What do you say, Billy?" The colonel asked the southerner standing next to him, "Shall we spare this man a hanging?"

"Suits me," the southerner said. "I think he's a witch-man. And therefore he should be burned like a witch."

"No!" gasped the saloonkeeper. "No I want—want to

125

be hanged! Please. This is the twentieth century!"

"Too late," Sturgis smiled. "After all, you cooked Van Patten, I think you should be cooked too. Bar-b-que style. Take him away Billy!" the Colonel said. "And make it fast. I want to blow this scene."

"I'll get my C.A.D.S suit—the men have been cleaning them. I'll use the LPF mode, colonel," Billy said. "Don't worry, it won't take but a few minutes."

As the Saloonkeeper was hustled away, Sturgis said, "I need a burial detail for the remains of our fallen comrades and for the cannibals. We dig up on that hill overlooking the town. Dig the cannibal graves shallow, and our guys' graves deep."

As the colonel stood at the top of "Boot Hill" supervising the burials, he heard the screams of the Saloonkeeper. He was tied to a stake back down in the town. And Billy was applying heat and flame slowly. Sturgis wondered what had ever got into him to allow Billy to torture the bastard. Torture, even torture of someone like the Saloonkeeper, was against his general practice. But nobody, not even the President, who had witnessed and approved the trials and hangings, had objected to his decision. They all wanted to let Billy have his way. Perhaps there are a few crimes that deserve the ultimate vengeance of torture!

Still, the colonel winced as he heard the screams of agony below. The screams that went on for a half hour and then ceased. And he didn't say a word when Billy pulled his tri-bike alongside the colonel and the southerner announced, "Bar-b-que over, sir."

Sturgis, after saying a brief prayer for the departed— some of whom were just soup bones when they had been buried—drew Renquist aside. "Sergeant," Sturgis said, "I'm gonna have to go back a bit on Billy's word to you.

126

Your men can't have all the spoils of battle. The U.S. government needs the high-tech equipment. We can't spare any tri's or C.A.D.S. suits."

"I understand, Colonel," the black man said. "All we want is replacement for our lost ammo, and a few necessities."

"Fine, we will leave you what ammo we can and supplies enough for your soldiers to tame this territory."

"Agreed—on one condition, Sturgis. My men can continue their work under my second in command, Munson. He distinguished himself today in combat, and deserves a promotion. I want him to take my place. Colonel, you mentioned that one of your C.A.D.S. men—Van Patten—was killed. That means you have an extra C.A.D.S. suit."

Sturgis smiled, "I get your drift. But it will take a while for you to learn how to use it. Are you a fast learner?"

"I can program a Jap VCR. Is that good enough?"

"It'll have to do, Renquist. I want you with us. I'll be proud to accept you as a recruit."

Sturgis gave the black officer a C.A.D.S. suit and fifteen minutes of instruction. Then he told the black man to take Van Patten's tri-bike. One of the White Sands recruited troopers, Jones, would ride along with Renquist, continuing Renquist's high-tech education.

Soon they all were leaving the hell-town. Morgana, significantly recovered, rode, holding on to Sturgis.

Their much delayed expedition to Fort Collins continued.

Chapter Eighteen

The expedition now moved rapidly. They were minus twenty-six members of the U.S. convoy that had fallen prey to the Saloonkeeper's madness.

When the convoy reached a rise that let the colonel see twenty miles in every direction under the sodden sky, Sturgis checked their position in three different ways. He calibrated with the geo-sensitive readout in the war-ambulance, and verified it with the sextant function *and* the old highway map. "There's no doubt about it, Tranh," he said to his second in command, "Fort Collins is less than thirty-one miles."

"That's what I have," Billy said. The colonel had ordered the southerner to do a separate check, using dead-reckoning.

Sturgis nodded. "We know where we are and we know where we're going. So let's go!" He silently wished that they could have veered off course and stopped at the Indian reservation. He was greatly concerned about Robin. Was she even still alive? Was she recovered?

But they had to reach the fort — before it was too late. And this was the quickest way. Securing the fort had to come first; establishing a new U.S. government base of operations. *Then* he would go to Robin. He revved up his tri-bike a bit higher, taking the lead.

All the colonel's systems were showing no sign of life nor any exhaust fumes in the direction of the subterranean fort. But then suddenly, there was a blip of unknown origin on his screen. It had suddenly appeared to the southeast. At first he had thought it a malfunction; but the blip didn't waver, nor did it go away.

"Skip," Billy reported, "My computer reads that blip as twenty-five men, and animals."

"I don't have that yet, Billy. Does anyone confirm?"

"Colonel," Fenton reported from the war-ambulance, "my readout defines them as riders on horseback."

Now Sturgis's computer finally came up with the same analysis. "Well, it isn't Reds. They don't have cavalry. We won't stop the column. I'll go up on my jets and have a look."

As Morgana waited on his tri, the colonel stepped away from it and fired his backpack jet-system. He rode up on a plume of smoke. At about a hundred feet up, leaning into the wind to keep above the convoy, he ordered the computer to fix the opti-scanner on telescope-mode. He peered intently at the image in his visor-screen.

Definitely a horde of riders to the southeast. But the image was unsteady, the heat and dust of the desert made them ill-defined. "Maximize gyro control," he said. "Computer, also correct for heat-distortion. Feed in radar mode to enhance image."

"Correcting . . ." the readout announced. And then the image became steady and clear, as if he was sitting in the air fifty feet from the mysterious riders. "Jesus!" the colonel exclaimed.

"What's up, Skip?" Tranh asked.

"They're Indians! I think it's our old friend Chief Naktu and some of his braves." Then Sturgis became silent. He saw a white woman among the riders. She was dressed in khakis, her long chestnut hair streaming in the wind. Sturgis's heart raced as the image of the woman became clearer. "My God, I think it's my wife, Robin," he exclaimed.

As the colonel jetted back down he said, "We will make a slight detour, thirty degrees southwest, to intercept the riders. I don't know what the hell they're doing out here. Maybe they had scouts out, and spotted us somehow."

The minutes passed like hours. When they came within a few miles' range of the Naqui Indians, the colonel saw a blinding flash from one of the riders. Then a rapid series of flashes. "Hold it up," he said, "they're sending us a message via hand held mirror. I can read it; it's in ordinary Morse code."

The colonel read it off: "Don't go any farther toward Fort Collins. Meet us at cave located twelve miles southwest. Now."

Sturgis wondered what the mirror-message was all about. He wished they had told him exactly what the danger was. But the message just kept repeating, until they altered course to head for the cave.

Fifteen minutes later the convoy reached the rendezvous. Just behind the Indian band, who had dismounted and taken up positions near the dark cavern entrance in a sheer rock cliff.

A few guard-Indians waved them on as they approached, evidently wanting the convoy to drive right into the level cavern entrance.

Sturgis hesitated. He didn't like going into some place he hadn't checked out. But then, before he could decide what to do, several braves approached on horseback from the cave. Chief Naktu, resplendent in his polished beer-can armor, was at their head.

"Sturgis," the chief yelled, "we have little time. Quickly, get everyone inside."

"What's up?"

"No time. We'll talk inside. Hurry." The chief reared his horse and turned, the braves followed. Sturgis raised his hand and motioned the convoy to follow, single file.

Once they were inside the torch-lit cavern, the chief dove off his horse and ran toward the colonel's bike. "Dean," he huffed, "your enemy has the fort. You have got to make new plans."

Sturgis grunted and got off his tri-bike, took off his helmet. He glanced around at the convoy personnel and Indians, then briefly noted the spiral chalk drawings and stick figures on the cavern walls. "Where is my wife? I saw her with your riders, and—" Sturgis began. And then she came to him, rushing into his arms. "Robin," he exclaimed, "you're all better."

"Thanks to our Indian friends and their natural remedies."

He swung her around, they hugged a long time, and then the chief touched his shoulder. "We have to talk," he insisted.

Sturgis sighed, gave Robin one more kiss and patted her on the backside, "Off, woman! I've got work to do." Sturgis let the chief lead him over to a natural rock shelf where they could sit more or less in private. When they had both seated themselves Indian-style, Sturgis asked, "Now what's this about the fort being in enemy hands? Are the Russians there?"

"No, not them! It is that traitor Pinky Ellis and his gang. They have seized the underground fortress. They lie in waiting for you. We watched for you from a ridge. We were waiting for you, hoping to prevent the trap from springing." The chief explained in brief: "Reverend Jerry Jeff Jeeters, together with a group of Appalachian freedom-fighters led by a boy named Chris, travelled west hoping to prevent you, Sturgis from being nuked at White Sands base. The eastern party had been delayed on their way west by Red patrols. Believing that they

131

were too late to warn you, Colonel, they diverted toward Fort Collins, when they picked up a signal from the fort to the Sov high command. That transmission told that Pinky Ellis had seized a magnificent underground base. Chris and Jeeters and the rest of the easterners were going to check out the situation at Fort Collins and try to do something about it.

"Then the eastern freedom fighters found our reservation. They were greeted as friends, fellow Americans, and joined forces with my Indians. Together we all rushed to near Fort Collins. I knew you would return there, if you survived the White Sands bombing. I wanted to stop you from walking into a trap. We were very lucky to catch you. Another few minutes and you would have been too close to the fort. Pinky's gang would have seen you."

"This is a lot to take in," Sturgis said. "But I thank you all. And you're right. We must have a new plan. Chief, I think that we *have to* get into that fort! If we can't take it over, then we have to blow it up." The colonel paused as a thin, pale man approached. The thin man was somehow familiar to Sturgis.

"Ah, excellent," the chief remarked upon seeing the man approach. "I am glad you have come over to listen to this discussion. Perhaps, Dean Sturgis, you recognize this gentleman from television?"

"Indeed I do; and it's a pleasure to meet the most famous preacher of all!" Sturgis stood and shook hands warmly with the infamous Jerry Jeff Jeeters, America's best spy. Then Chris came over. "We've met before, Colonel" said the teenage lad. "It's good to find you're still alive."

"The feeling is mutual," Sturgis replied. For a long time, Chris had been the one person who had kept Robin alive. (see CADS #2) And Sturgis would never forget that fact.

The four sat down and they tossed around ideas for what to do about what was, in essence, an impossible situation. First, Sturgis filled the Indian, Chris and the reverend in on what had happened at White Sands, and how the President was alive but ill, lying in the war-ambulance. He spoke little about their troubles along the way, troubles like the cannibal-village. The colonel just said they had been "delayed" on their way to the fort.

"You were saying," the chief asked, "that if we get into the fort and fail to take it over, we could blow it up. How, Colonel?"

"The whole fort receives its power supply from a self-regulating nuclear core down at the lowest level," Sturgis explained. "It can be reached by a tunnel denoted as 'tunnel 333.' Here," Sturgis said, pulling out a mini-blueprint of part of the fort from his belt pack. He had acquired the drawing during his quick visit to Fort Collins, before the trek to White Sands. (see CADS #7)

They all studied the plan, and it soon became obvious that they'd need a virtual army of fighters to secure the fort while a sapper went down tunnel 333 and pulled out the control rods. Even then, there wouldn't be enough time to evacuate their forces from the fort before the nuclear power source exploded.

"We don't have a chance of pulling an attack off," Chris said. "The traitor has been in the fort for a few days now. There are endless supplies and armaments in there. Pinky must have a vast arsenal at his command now, and good surveillance capability as well. It's just luck that we caught your convoy out of range of his detectors. We'd never be able to infiltrate a *flea*. Besides, even if we could get in, we couldn't keep control. That traitor probably has men all over that fort. We'd be at a great disadvantage."

"I want that fort as the new U.S. base of operations," Sturgis insisted.

Chief Naktu stood up and said, "I say we pull back for now. We should head back to the reservation. We'll need well-conceived plan of attack and many men. Plus more ammo. Maybe we can figure out how to use those missiles that my braves found in the storehouse near there. With those missiles we will be able to seize the fort and not blow it up."

"What's this about missiles, chief?" Sturgis asked, encouraged. "And why didn't you bring them along?"

The Indian sighed. "Old Stinger missiles, and a few Lance air-to-air jobs. Maybe fifteen. Very heavy. We didn't bring them along, because we had to make speed. We didn't know if we could figure out how to launch them anyway."

"Our computers can analyze any equipment," Sturgis said. "You have an idea there. If we can get those missiles operational, we can blast our way into Fort Collins. They won't be expecting such firepower."

Sturgis noticed now that Robin was staring across at them from where the Indian squaws and she were sitting on the opposite side of the cavern. Morgana was sitting right next to her! The look Robin shot him indicated to the colonel that the two women had just had quite a conversation concerning him. Was that an *angry* look?

The parlay broke up, once all agreed that Chief Naktu had the best idea. As Sturgis went over to tell his forces the decision, Robin and Morgana both approached him. Double trouble?

He tried to look too busy to talk. But as Sturgis got his men mounted up and shouted out orders, Robin whispered in his ear, "It's okay, darling. We have decided that we'll share you."

His ears burned and his heart did flip flops as he nodded and kissed them both lightly on their cheeks. Then he closed his visor and mounted his tri. Robin got on behind him, and Morgana took the seat behind

Tranh, who rode alongside his commander's vehicle. They both gave the high-sign.

The Indian warriors rode out of the cavern first, followed by the tri's, with the convoy trucks and the war-wagon-ambulance last. As they all roared across the barren desert terrain, Robin managed to convey a few more words before it got too noisy. "I told Morgana that I didn't mind her sleeping with you, Dean. We are going to be friends. War makes you very practical."

Sturgis felt dizzy and dry in the mouth, but said, "That's good." But he wasn't sure at all that it was possible for him to manage a set-up like this! Besides, there was another matter to attend to: Saving the United States of America from total destruction!

Chapter Nineteen

The convoy, led by the Indian riders, moved like the devil toward the reservation. But it was soon evident to the colonel that the valiant effort of the Revengers and the Indians to warn them had been in vain. Up in the sky Sturgis saw several small metal cylinders with slender wings wheeling around, like vultures. The suit-computer identified them as U.S.-made devices. Not bombs, but surveillance cameras! And their point of origin was Fort Collins!

"Pink's on to us," the colonel exclaimed, "we've got to make faster time."

The chief, who had been equipped with a walkie-talkie by the colonel, responded from atop his horse at the head of the retreat-column, "My riders will fall back, and try to slow them. Push your vehicles up to their fastest speed."

Sturgis made the decision to stick close to the President. Defend him to the last. "Thanks for the offer, Chief, but the President is in the war-wagon ambulance, and it's unable to keep up a tri-bike's one hundred fifty mph. Besides, they'll soon be on us. Now that we're spotted, we'd better prepare for an attack." He didn't feel it inside his C.A.D.S. suit, of course, but the readouts showed that Robin's grip on his waist had tightened. She knew things didn't look good.

"Billy, do you copy this conversation?" Sturgis radioed.

No response. The war-ambulance didn't have a very good com system. Sturgis cursed and slowed to drop his tri-bike back. Soon he was alongside the war-wagon ambulance, and hand-signaled Billy, who had relieved Fenton at the wheel of the big vehicle, to switch to a broad-beam channel.

Billy's voice now came on loud and clear. "What's up, Skip?"

"Billy, we have company. Surveillance aircraft. Prepare your anti-air weapons systems."

"You want I should shoot down the surveillance craft, right?"

"You could try, pal. Probably they've got countermeasures. But try!"

Billy got right to it, and he fired several ground to air Destructor missiles from the war-wagon ambulance. They shot upward with a roar, covering the area with hot black smoke for a second. As the colonel expected, the missiles suddenly veered. They had been deflected in mid-flight, and blew up once they were several miles away. "Electronic countermeasures are too effective, Billy. Nice shot, though."

"Skip?" Billy asked, "if the enemy can see us out here, why aren't they—"

As if to answer the southerner, there came a series of rumbling burps—noises coming from the direction of the fort. "Those were explosions, not someone's artillery," Sturgis said, perplexed. "What the hell is going on?" Then he realized the computer might know. "Computer: identify noises bearing one hundred eighty degrees back."

The computer identified the noises as: "CONCRETE COVERS OF SEALED DOORWAYS BLOWING OFF."

Doors blowing off? Sturgis was mystified. Why? What on earth was coming out of the underground fort that couldn't come through the fifty-foot-wide door that Sturgis and his men had seen when they discovered Fort Collins just a month earlier?

The colonel soon found out! The convoy was moving up a slaggy rise now, and the rearview telemode he accessed showed Sturgis a jumping image of the fort area. And he saw that huge gouges had appeared in the smooth earth. And out of those ugly scars were pouring forth gleaming objects. They were a hundred feet in length each; three of them.

Billy, who had also picked up the objects on his rear-detector, asked, "Skip, what the hell are those things? They look like shiny metal ants." And as he said this, the shiny objects started to rise off the ground.

"Computer," Sturgis ordered, "define three metallic objects, bearing one hundred eighty."

Immediately, his helmet readout stated: "OBJECTS ARE A-23A MODEL BANDERSNATCH-CLASS FLOATING AIR-TANKS."

Sturgis groaned. He'd been up against smaller air-tanks before, in New Orleans. And half his men had been killed. Now there were three big versions of them! "Computer," he exclaimed, "identify pursuing weapons armament-systems."

"SHIELDED WEAPONS SYSTEMS CANNOT BE ANALYZED," the computer stated. "BUT I COULD GUESS."

Sturgis, raising one eyebrow at the computer's unusual offer, said, "Okay, guess."

"BANDERSNATCH-CLASS TANKS OF THIS CONFIGURATION ARE USUALLY ARMED WITH NQ-5 TWIN LASERS AND .56 CALIBER EXPLOSIVE-SHELL SMG. PLUS TWO HAWK ANTI-MISSILE SYSTEMS EACH. SMG SYSTEMS CONTAIN TWELVE-HUNDRED-ROUND MAGAZINES, EACH CAPABLE OF—"

"Cancel," Sturgis said, wanting more than a shopping

list of horrors. "Computer, list possible countermoves for our force. State best strategic positioning."

"WORKING . . . NO VIABLE COUNTER MEASURES," the computer replied, not the least bit excited that it was reading Sturgis and the U.S. government-in-exile their *death warrants*.

"PROBABILITY OF DESTRUCTION ONE HUNDRED PERCENT," the computer stated before Sturgis could order, "Cancel."

Billy, who had been sharing the info with the colonel on his tie-in, raged, "How can the damned computer be one hundred percent sure?"

Sturgis said nothing. He was concentrating on developing a solution to the totally hopeless situation. Computers don't know everything. For instance, they can't understand the principle called bluff. Sturgis decided the convoy should pretend that it was preparing to defend itself, even if that was an impossibility. The enemy might move more cautiously if the C.A.D.S. unit looked like they were doing *something*. He decided to form a circle, and he ordered the unit and the trucks into that configuration. He told the pony riders to get inside the metal circle of trucks and tri-bikes.

The unmanned surveillance aircraft had now flown away. And coming in low and slow—like some old German dirigibles from World War Two—came several of the Bandersnatch air-tanks. There were three of the glistening high-tech cylinders, boxing the colonel's newly formed circle, coming in at them slowly from all sides. It was positively surreal, he thought. The air-tanks were nearly silent. They floated on their humming anti-grav devices fifty feet off the desert floor like giant metal ghosts. Soon, there were portals opening on all sides of the craft. Gun-ports.

"Fire now," Sturgis commanded his men. "Aim for their gun ports. Use manual-overrides. Fire whatever

you guess might work. Ignore what your computers say."
(After all, the computer said it was hopeless. He never
paid attention to a defeatist!)

The C.A.D.S. unit fired everything they had: Electro-
balls, mini-missiles, smg's, even the grapple-darts. The
back-wash from the combined force of hundreds of exploding shells and Electro-balls exploding so close to
them nearly blasted off the colonel's helmet. Sturgis
shielded Robin with his bulk, but he worried about her
and anyone not wearing a metal suit. The Indians, their
horses falling or bolting away, fell from their mounts
under the barrage. Damage had already been done,
without the enemy firing a shot!

The air-tanks hadn't been damaged at all! The Bandersnatches now moved off a bit, though, and began
circling. It was like Conestoga wagons in the sky, Sturgis
thought wryly for a second. Sky-wagons circling Indians
and their friends. A weird turn-around to the old-west
scene!

Then he had no more time for such thoughts. For the
air-tanks started firing. Just bullets—but highly accu-
rate fire. The bullets snapped into the ground just in
front of the C.A.D.S. men. A warning salvo. A chance to
surrender, perhaps.

"Bloody hell, what do we do now, Skip?" Fenton asked.

"Anybody have any ideas?" the colonel asked.

"I remember something about the air-tanks' vulnera-
bility," Fireheels replied. "I stopped the one in New
Orleans by pulling out wires. I jumped on its roof to do
that, remember?"

"Can't do that now," Tranh said calmly. "Notice the red
glow on top of them? Near their hatches? That's some
kind of a deadly repel-system, according to my analysis.
It's deadly, even in a C.A.D.S. suit."

"Thanks for the info," the Indian-trooper said. "I was
just planning to play the hero and climb up there!"

140

Now the Bandersnatches were setting up a spray of fire, just more bullets, and these too were aimed short of the circle of defense.

"They aren't firing anything big, Skip. Why?" asked Rossiter.

"I figure that Pinky wants us alive. To steal our equipment, maybe torture us all for info. Dead, we'd be lots less useful."

Then the booming ultimatum came out of all the air-tanks simultaneously: "THIS IS DISCIPLE QP-5, OF THE COMBINED GLORIOUS ARMIES OF THE NEW AMERICA. YOU WILL ALL IMMEDIATELY GIVE UP. DROP YOUR WEAPONS AND TAKE OFF YOUR COMBAT SUITS. SURRENDER AND YOU WILL NOT BE HARMED."

The amplification nearly burst their eardrums.

"What the hell," Billy asked, "is all that stuff about 'combined forces', Skip?"

"Who knows!" Sturgis said. "In any case, this is the end of the road. We will go down fighting."

The colonel turned and looked at Robin, and said, "Sorry honey, for getting you into this mess. You know we can't surrender."

"I know. And it doesn't matter," she said. "The world is too awful to go on now, anyway. Better to die here, with you. I love you," she said.

"And I love you."

The colonel was about to shout up, "No dice, shitheads," and then he had an idea, based upon information about the high-tech weapons they had discovered in New Orleans. "Computer," he asked, "what about the air tanks' fuel capacity? What is their range?"

"RESTATE QUESTION." The computer was getting picky in its old age!

Sturgis screamed, "Damn it! Compute range stats for air-vehicles attacking."

"BANDERSNATCH RANGE TEN MILES. MAXIMUM OPERAT-

The colonel's mind raced. The enemy were anxious for a surrender. They wouldn't fire to kill, not for a few more minutes anyway! He hadn't figured out a bluff that would work, but maybe if he stalled for time, the tanks would run out of fuel! Perhaps, just perhaps the assholes Pinky had flying the air-tanks hadn't had time to check out the stats of their high-tech babies!

The colonel walked forward and then said on all radio-frequencies, "We are willing to negotiate a surrender agreement . . ." He went on to list a whole set of demands, not expecting them to be met, but just to keep talking.

He received several long-winded replies as to why they had to surrender immediately and unconditionally. But by then, the colonel's stall started to work wonders! Sturgis saw the lead air-tank losing altitude. It started to nose over. With all its stabilizer jets firing, it was unable to prevent itself from plowing nose first into the desert sands. Out of gas!

Now the second and third Bandersnatch collapsed to the desert, hitting hard enough to rupture their metal-skins and start burning up. Men — some on fire — were running from the crashed vessels. Some were in khakis, and some wore white robes. A few bursts of smg fire from the C.A.D.S. unit killed all those who managed to escape their death inside the burning air-tanks.

"Let's move out," Sturgis ordered triumphantly, starting up his big tri-bike. "Let's get outta here before — "

But before any action to leave could be effected, there were noises — loud rumbling noises.

Fenton, who was at the top of the rise on his tri-bike scanning the fort-area shouted, "Skip! Ground vehicles coming. Big mothers — armor-loaded."

Sturgis sighed. The enemy already was following up the ineffective air-tank attack. "What's our analysis say?

Can we outrun them, Fenton?"

"Negative, Skip. These are N-class jobbies. Can make the same speed as our bikes. But unlike the air-tanks, they can be destroyed by E-balls and by direct hit of missiles."

"Then we stay and fight."

Chapter Twenty

The two dozen rapidly approaching enemy ground-vehicles were already firing howitzer-type shells at the colonel's forces. The shells arched up at steep angles, and were heading, according to computer analysis, directly at the center of the U.S. convoy. They were not warning shots. These babies were meant to utterly decimate. The firepower of the squat, camouflage-painted Fort Collins armored vehicles was awesome. A rain of death approached.

But the colonel had some firepower of his own. "Men," he shouted, "fire surface to air counter measures from your tri-systems!"

As ordered, the unit of nuke-troopers shot their defensive barrage up at the incoming shells, a whooshing hail of small missiles that brought the barrage to nil. The enemy shells were destroyed in mid-air, concussion after concussion from the blasts shaking the ground.

But there would soon be another volley, and then another and another. It was inevitable that some shells would reach target. And those not protected by the C.A.D.S. suits would surely die.

The colonel ordered the Electro-balls, the ace-in-the-hole weapons of the unit, fired at the approaching tanks. The E-balls flew fast and furious at the enemy, and exploded on target—without effect.

And the enemy returned fire, hit two trucks. And the trucks were destroyed. Along with their dozen occupants. Sturgis realized that there had been children in those convoy vehicles.

Echoing the commander's unspoken horror, Fenton stated, "Skip, this has to stop! These damned new mini-E-Balls we've been provided with by the geniuses back at White Sands are worth *shit!* And we'll run out of other ammo before the enemy does, that's for sure."

"What the hell can we do except keep firing?" Rossiter replied. "We've used up our options. We're doomed this time."

Sturgis's mind raced like a speeding tri-bike. He said, "Maybe not, Rossiter. I've had my computer analyzing the enemy's response time—the amount of time they take to re-calibrate our range and fire their salvos. If we stop trying to run and we turn on them, the analysis indicates that will throw them off for a few seconds. If we can get back to the ridge, bear down on them, fire our complete inventory from there, we *might* knock 'em out."

"One last burst of glory?" Rossiter criticized, "Sure, why not Skip? Why not go out in a blaze of glory? Why drag it out?" Hysteria edged the worn-to-a-frazzle commando's voice.

Sturgis ignored the comment and said, "Prepare to reverse course—tight turn to the left—on my command. . . . *Now!*"

The shells arching up this time were not met by C.A.D.S.-fire. No need to fire. The shells flew overhead and impacted where they would have been.

They were fifty yards from the ridge, twenty . . . and then Sturgis pulled his tri-bike up. "God Almighty," he whispered to himself as he saw that there were at least fifty of the huge attack-tanks down in the valley. No way were they going to knock all of *those* out. Still, when he cried out, "Give 'em all you got," there was a certain delicious pride in those words. At least, as Rossiter said, they would go out in a blaze of glory!

The entire convoy eagerly complied with the colonel's order. E-balls flew like roman candles from the firing tubes of the troopers' kill-suits. A rainbow array of explosive bullets, darts, missiles, flew down upon the enemy like a rain of judgment from the gods of the mountain. As the enemy guns burped out their death-songs, they were hit by dozens of the shots from the ridge. Two of the enemy crawl-vehicles were blasted to their dirt-clogged treads, flaming bodies sent up into the air like embers from an exploding fireplace log.

It was the C.A.D.S. unit's minihawk missiles that did the most damage. Another ten of the fifty death-machines below erupted into bloody flaming shrapnel.

Alas, the U.S. force did not have enough firepower to finish the job. The colonel's men, though they made the most of what they had, were soon out of ammo. As the last click of the C.A.D.S. unit's empty systems magazines sounded, there was a sudden silence from the enemy force as well.

"The enemy is withholding fire," Fenton gasped. "Why?"

"Obviously, we're being given another chance to surrender," the colonel said grimly. There were heavy casualties among the civilians.

"What do we do?" Billy asked "Do we try to run again?"

"I don't know," Sturgis mumbled. "Just sit tight. Try to take care of the wounded. We'll listen to their offer."

"Surrender?" Billy snarled. "I'd much rather die fighting. We can go down there, Skip. We can use our suit servo-power to rip open their tanks and take them on hand to hand."

"I'm for that," the chief said. Sturgis saw that the Indian's hook-nosed, tawny face was all bloody. But the half-naked warrior still had his tomahawk up. "Sturgis, lead the charge. I can use a few traitor-scalps. Let us go down honorably. As Chief Crazy Horse once said, 'today is a good day to die.' "

"We'd never get a yard," Sturgis said. "Billy, consult your computer tracking-mode. We're being scanned."

"If we go either way," Billy said, "forward or back, they're ready to pour it on again."

They just waited. The silence was deafening. Finally, one of the behemoth tanks boomed out a message: "You have five minutes to decide. Surrender unconditionally or die."

It was up to Sturgis. He knew they were defenseless. A quick reference to the computer I.D. Mode listed the names of the troopers who had fallen. Twelve C.A.D.S. men in all. Including the new trooper, Sergeant Renquist. Torn-open C.A.D.S. suits littered the ground all around him, testament to the fact that the tanks' shells could rip open the rest of the C.A.D.S. units in seconds. The toll on the unarmored parts of the colonel's convoy were more grievous: the enemy had already made mincemeat of two-thirds of the Indian braves, and the trucks of the convoy were half destroyed. Casualties among the civvies and Appalachian freedom-fighters over fifty percent. The colonel bit his lip. There's got to be another way, other than surrender. What? What for God's sake could he do? He spent the last few minutes pondering that question.

"Your time is up," the enemy mike boomed out. Clouds of dust and smoke raised by the battle was still partially obscuring the area. Neither side could see the other group well.

Sturgis broadcast on a wide channel, so that the enemy would pick up his reply. "We surrender. Men, you heard what I said.—Start walking slowly toward the tanks."

There were a lot of moans and shouts of "no" on his communicator, right after that. "Switch to secret channel five," the colonel said. Once the unit did so, he said, "I'm not really surrendering, gang. I have a plan. Play along like we're surrendering. We have a better chance of winning once we're inside the fort."

"What's the plan, Skip?" Fireheels asked, as the C.A.D.S. unit and then the convoy slowly moved down toward the enemy tanks.

Sturgis said, "We know some of Fort Collins's layout. And I have a wild idea! They probably don't know about Jerry Jeff Jeeters being on *our* side. Pinky — I hope — only knows of Jerry as a traitor to the U.S. cause. The bastard might welcome Jeeters, if we make the reverend appear to be a prisoner of ours. Jerry, are you picking this up on your earphones?"

A much distorted reply came crackling over the little head set. "Copy, Colonel. A good idea. It's worth a try. What do I do?"

"First, let Chris hold a gun on you. — Got that Chris? And tie the reverend's hands. Quick, do it while you're obscured by all the dust."

Chris responded, "I copy, Colonel."

When the dust cloud raised by the tank force moved away, Sturgis saw the teen freedom-fighter had moved into position holding a rifle against the newly bound reverend.

"Good. Now, Jerry," the colonel said, with tension edging his rapid remarks, "with your bravery, Jeeters, and with your spy-ability, you can be our inside man. You play-act the part of the arch-traitor against democracy. And then —"

"CHANNEL SIGNAL BEING SCANNED," the computer reported. And a warning light came on inside Sturgis's helmet. The enemy had accessed the secret channel. The colonel could say no more. He'd have to hope that Jerry could 'wing it.' Without a pause, the colonel switched the nature of his words so that the enemy would think he had been talking of something else. He said: "So I'm sorry men, but surrender is the only way that America will live. That's why I asked you all to be brave and surrender with me. There are three hundred thirty-three ways to die and only one way to live . . ." (Sturgis hoped that the reverend caught the reference to tunnel 333 in the fort — the tunnel that led to the nuke-reactor that could blow the place sky-high.) "We have to give up," the colonel continued, "so that the wounded can be treated, and so that our women and children can live. We must trust the generosity of our captor. He is, after all, an American like we are . . ."

The "surrendering Americans" now reached the tanks. And the speaker on the lead tank boomed out again. The voice now was clearer, and its squeaky grating essence was familiar as hell to the colonel. "This is Emperor Pinky Ellis. I have been monitoring your secret channel," Pinky chuckled. "And your words are wise. You are wise to surrender, Colonel. No one will be hurt — and the wounded will be treated well. Come on now. Follow this tank back in. In case you're wondering — I'm not in this vehicle. It is, you see, a totally remote controlled device. A robot device — one of many wonderful toys I found in the fort. It will guide you into the fort for a nice meal and some entertainment. All is forgiven. I bear no grudges over past problems between the C.A.D.S. unit and my forces."

"I'll bet," Billy said, caustically. The colonel knew that Billy was remembering how he had once left the fat traitor Pinky Ellis up to his neck in an ant hill. (see CADS #3) Billy knew that torture was probably the fate of the entire leadership of the C.A.D.S. force. Pinky never forgave anyone. He *got even*.

"Please, gentlemen, raise your hands," Sturgis announced, "and follow the tank back into the fort."

As soon as the speaker went dead, the tank had turned around on its thick treads and began to move toward the fort.

"Say your prayers, men," Sturgis added dryly. "And raise your hands high over your heads. We're going to do as Pinky says. Follow his tank into the fortress, offer no resistance."

The decimated force of C.A.D.S. men and their companions followed Pinky's armor-vehicle, flanked on all sides by the rest of the tanks. A wall of deadly steel around a badly mauled group of supposedly defeated Americans.

Sturgis, seeing a mass of mercenary soldiers with blood-lust in their eyes pouring out of hatch-entrances to the fort, wondered if this was such a bright idea after all.

Chapter Twenty-one

The huge lead tank reached a giant hatchway leading downward into a dark corridor. This was yet another entrance into the vast underground fortress known as Fort Collins.

"Prisoners will follow this vehicle inside," the speakers of the tank boomed out. "Once inside, the C.A.D.S. unit will remove their armor suits. The suits will be collected by our forces.

"Skip," Billy asked, "what do we—"

"We do as they say," the colonel ordered.

Soon, the sound of explosive bolts popping open the suits followed. Sturgis felt the harsh desert heat pouring down. He looked at his dissembled high-tech C.A.D.S. unit mournfully and then stepped forward feeling naked as a jaybird in his sweaty black coveralls. The speaker told them all to walk slowly, hands up, toward the enemy soldiers.

There were literally hundreds of smg armed men swarming around the enclosure. There were skinny, wide eyed bastards, dressed in white robes, and some khaki-clad beefy types too.

Martel moved closer to the colonel as they stepped forward and whispered, "Skip, what the hell are these guys in robes? What kind of soldiers wear robes?"

Sturgis frowned and out of the corner of his mouth mumbled, "Some seem to be dressed like the cultists our unit encountered a while back—remember I told you about Anetra and the Cult of the White Light?"

"Do I!—You told me how Anetra committed suicide rather than surrender. She's dead, and I thought you killed most of them. Are the cultists part of Pinky's traitor band now?"

"Looks that way. I guess the leaderless remnants of her force joined up with Pinky's outfit, somewhere."

There was no more time for talk. The prisoners were surrounded and searched quickly, then shoved at gun point toward a staircase.

"Why is this man tied?" one of the robed bastards asked, his eyes narrowing, his smg pointing at Chief Naktu's gut. "Why are you leading him on a rope, Injun?"

The chief said nothing but Jeeters spoke up, "Comrade," he gasped out, "I am on your side. I am a prisoner. I demand to be released now and taken to whoever is in charge. I am Reverend Jeeters, I am famous. He will know—"

"Hmmph. I do think I recognize you. Pinky will want to talk to you. But for now, you stay with these men. We will sort this out later."

As the men were herded forward, the chief spoke up. "Hey, what about the horses? You can't just leave 'em here, without food or water. Look at them—they are pitiful. Some are wounded."

Someone who had evidently been listening from afar now shouted orders on a speaker in the ceiling. It was a woman's voice. She spoke in a strange tongue, but the cultists seemed to understand her. They stuck out their hands in a modified "Sieg heil," and then they lifted their smg's and mowed down the frenzied Indian ponies that had come down the ramp.

When the whinnying death calls died down, the cultist in charge snapped out, "Now get going, Injun. All of you — *march!*"

"Just like sheep going to slaughter," Billy said disconsolately between clenched teeth. "We're probably next to die."

They were forced to ascend the wide stair that led the captives up onto a wide esplanade inside the fort. It was a huge area that Sturgis had not seen on his brief survey of the fort a month earlier.

Here the white-light cultists were outnumbered by the hard looking filthy khaki clad men — Pinky's army of mercenaries, no doubt. They carried sidearms as well as smg's.

Sturgis quickly looked around and was satisfied that there were no Russians around. That was good; very good. The colonel's plan of destruction depended on that fact.

Sturgis realized he had never eyeballed this part of Fort Collins before. The fortress was apparently even more vast than he had thought.

Now they were told to stand still and look at the far wall, where a giant visi-screen was lowering. The screen soon lit up with the face of a fat jowled man with wispy hair who wore a pink Nehru-style jacket. Pinky Ellis!

Quickly Sturgis gave the reverend the eye and Jeeters did his thing. The clergyman tore away from the chief, who still held his rope, and came forth among the enemy. "Emperor Pinky," he shouted, "I told your men, but they wouldn't listen! I'm Reverend Jeeters, loyal subject of the Soviet empire! You must know me! They — the C.A.D.S. men — captured me," the reverend implored, staring up at the huge visi-screen filled with Pinky's face. "Thank God you came along to rescue me!"

Sturgis's guess that the visi-screen was two-way was confirmed as the giant fat face of Pinky seemed to move closer to the camera and look down at the reverend. And then Pinky's image smiled. "Ah, yes. It is the famous Jerry Jeff Jeeters, is it not?"

"Yes, it's me! Please release me."

"Of course," Pinky said. "Honor guards! Come forth! Take that man and untie him. Bring the reverend to me."

"Traitor! Pig," some of the C.A.D.S. men began shouting. "We should have killed you," they yelled as Jeeters was untied.

"Thank you, Emperor Pinky," Jeeters said as he rubbed his freed wrists. The silver helmeted honor guard saluted him.

"Take the reverend to hospitality suite three," Pinky boomed out. "See that he's fed and entertained as he wishes, until I have time to speak with him."

The pair of honor guards saluted stiff armed, like Nazis, at Pinky's looming image. And then they escorted the smiling waving "collaborator" toward a gold doored elevator. Jeeters and the guards got in and the door closed.

They really don't know he's one of us, Sturgis thought, with relief. The plan was going to work! Reverend Jeeters, roaming free, would wreak terrible vengeance. He would destroy all of it!

One by one the prisoners were brought to a place on the floor marked by an X. That was evidently where Jeeters had stood, a place where Pinky could observe the prisoners from his vantage point. The fat traitor greeted Sturgis and each of the "Inner Group" of the C.A.D.S. unit by name and told them they would be treated "especially well" with a sinister smirk. When Pinky saw Morgana, his voice boomed out. "Ah, sweet victory! Fate has again brought us together. I believed you had died, my sweet. I'm very surprised to see you. But you needn't spit up at me like that. You see, you are nothing to me anymore. Your attempts at rejection are in vain! It is I who now reject you. You're not wanted any more, Morgana. You are not privileged to have my affection any more."

"Pig," she shouted up. "You'll get yours."

"Indeed I already have, Morgana, gotten mine! I am in charge here at the mightiest fort in the universe. And I now have a blissful arrangement now. You will soon see! Guards, take her to our throne room." He added, "You'd better also bring along Sturgis and his wife Robin. That is Robin in the buckskin outfit, isn't it?"

"No, that's not my wife," Sturgis said, knowing that if Pinky knew who she was, he would treat Robin especially badly.

"So you say," Pinky laughed. "But we have means of identifying her."

"The President needs medical care," Sturgis insisted, to change the subject. He pointed to the stretcher-borne man.

"Yes, I suppose he does. I suppose I should make sure Williamson stays alive. I will want to turn him over to my Soviet allies."

Pinky ordered a medical team to come forth and take the President, and only the President, to the hospital unit. "Leave those other sick and wounded alone," he smirked. "Let them suffer."

"Bastard!" Sturgis said between his teeth. But at least the President would be treated well. For now, he'd be safe.

Sturgis, Robin and Morgana were separated from the others and they were manhandled into the elevator. They rapidly descended many floors.

"Where are we going," he asked the stoic-looking guards.

"To the Imperial throne room," the man on the right snapped.

"Throne room?" Sturgis had to laugh. "Throne room?

155

Your leader is mad as a hatter!"

"Silence!"

The elevator door finally opened and trumpets blared in Sturgis's ears. Men in bejewelled white, robes emblazoned with pink trim, were playing those trumpets, and they weren't very good. "You'd better stop playing," Sturgis shouted, "unless you guys have union cards!"

The trumpeters, looking sheepish, stopped their awful wail.

The curtain of red before the captives was now opened, held back by two turbanned men in white robes. Sturgis and Morgana and Robin were shoved along down the long pink runner, toward a blue curtain.

And when that concealing curtain was pulled back, Sturgis saw two figures seated before him, raised up on a white marble — no, plastic — throne. The figure on the right wearing a king's crown was Pinky Ellis. That was bad enough. But Sturgis gasped as he took in the equally rotund figure on the left. His jaw opened wide in amazement, for sitting on the left throne, all dressed up in purple taffeta was —

"Anetra!" the colonel gasped. "You're alive!"

Chapter Twenty-two

Anetra laughed long and hard. A shrill laugh that convulsed her mass of fat and sent it jiggling like a bowl of jello. "You are no doubt surprised," she said finally, "that I am here? Well, it takes more than a little fire to put me out of business." She laughed again. "The joke's on you, Sturgis. How could you be so naive? You thought I died when I plunged into the flames of eternity back in Iowa, didn't you? (see CADS #5) That act was all part of my escape plan. Beneath the flames was a tunnel and my nice red sports car, in which I made my escape. You and your tech-troopers might have destroyed my operations there, but you couldn't destroy the great Anetra, Goddess of Atlantis. And now, fate has brought us together again, my dear Colonel. How quaint." She leaned over and kissed Pinky on his left jowl. "Pinky and I have joined forces, as you have probably surmised. We two are lovers, and soon we will be man and wife—or rather, Emperor and Empress."

"Yes," Pinky emoted, smiling like a sick puppy in heat, "together Anetra and I will rule this country, and eventually the whole world. Why not?"

Anetra giggled when Pinky squeezed her fat hand.

Sturgis said, "How nice for you two to have found each other. Sort of like the way two turds sink to the same level

157

in the toilet. And as for your idea of ruling America together, I think your Russian masters, Pinky, will not like that idea. Besides, America is not finished yet."

Anetra rose, red faced. "How *dare* you insult this throne! Now you will kneel before us, all three of you! Then we might question you. You will all answer our questions before we put you to death!"

"Get stuffed," Morgana blurted out. "Oh, I guess that's impossible, you're both already stuffed."

"Silence!" Pinky yelled. "Guards, force that woman to her knees. Force them all down to their knees. They will not defy us."

The whips flew and massive hands pushed down on their shoulders. The colonel and the women went down at last onto their knees.

Pinky rose and walked all around Morgana. "You little bitch! You know, I once desired you more than anyone or anything in the world, Morgana. How could I be so foolish? You are not of my kind. You are a sheep, not a wolf. You are not at all like Anetra. But I am happy to say that mistake of mine is over now. Morgana, you now mean nothing to me. I shall perhaps give you to one of my officers as a pleasure toy. I have one particularly sadistic officer in mind . . . Krantz! Come here at once."

From the ranks of braid- and gold-bedecked officers around the thrones now stepped a warty-faced "officer." Krantz was, the colonel saw, a very tall and very ugly man. He had several huge zig-zag scars on his face. Krantz saluted and he smiled as Pinky Ellis told him, "Take Morgana away and have some pleasure with her."

The colonel was restrained from helping her resist. Morgana was pulled along the marble floor, having been knocked unconscious by Krantz.

"Krantz has peculiar tastes," Pinky said, kissing his new love Anetra full on the lips. The kiss lasted a long time. Spittle drooled down their chins before they stopped their obscene osculation.

"Now, we deal with the wife of Dean Sturgis," Pinky smirked. "Perhaps you would like to disrobe before us, Robin, and show us what is so attractive about you that America's foremost soldier would have the hots for you?"

"Never," Robin said. But there was a tense edge in her voice. She knew that Pinky was able to make her comply. She added defiantly, "Besides, I don't have enough blubber on my body to turn you on, Shitface."

Pinky stood up red-faced, enraged at the defiance. "Fool! Don't you know," he snapped, "what I can do to you? An emperor has ultimate power. Power of life and death and power of torture."

"Leave her alone!" Sturgis hissed and he tried to stand. He was shoved down on his knees again by a dozen rough hands.

"Ah, that's better," Pinky said. "I was beginning to think you cared more for the other woman than your wife. Well well, now how can I exploit your desire to save this woman? Perhaps I will let her live, if you tell me all about the positions of U.S. Forces, and all the secrets of the C.A.D.S. suits. Start talking, Colonel. Respect my power, and maybe . . . we can work a deal."

"Maybe you can make me bow, Pinky, but you can't make me respect a traitor. You wouldn't honor a deal, because you have no honor. You have nothing to offer. You're no emperor. You're a poseur, a turncoat ball of lard."

"Ah, you wish to be punished, do you? As well as to watch your wife be punished? Well, we know how to make that a *shattering* experience, don't we, Anetra, dear?" he winked. Pinky turned to Sturgis again, and raised his voice, "Speak now, Colonel, spill your guts out. Or we will deal with your wife right now, right before your eyes. Tell us where the other U.S. forces are, what their battle plans are. Tell us the secrets of the C.A.D.S.

suits. Give us the codes to operate the suits."

Sturgis said nothing. He strained at his bindings for all he was worth, and they didn't budge. His only hope was that Jeeters was doing something now. Something to reverse this very serious situation.

The fat traitoress now snapped her finger and one of her gold robed lackeys came forth. "Pod 97," she intoned, "go fetch the 'sprayer'."

He bowed and moved off backward, continuing to bow until he was out of the room. "Sturgis," Anetra said, "We have discovered many fine new toys in this fortress. One of them is what is known as a Zero-Kelvin Sprayer. We will freeze-dry this bitch of yours before your eyes, if you don't cooperate."

Sturgis still said nothing. In a short while, the lackey returned, pushing a hand-cart with a strange vacuum-cleaner type device on it.

Anetra said, "Pod 97, now you will show the colonel that we mean business. Use the sprayer on this rose, first, so that he will see the horror that is to befall his wife." She took a rose from a vase and held the redolent red blossom forth. The "Pod" took it from her and placed it on the marble floor. Then he went over to the device on the cart and lifted the hose-like part of it, and flicked a switch.

Nothing happened. It just got a bit colder in the room. Then the lackey put the nozzle of the hose up against the rose. And the rose frosted over.

"Cease," Anetra said. "It is done." Sturgis wondered what the hell she meant until Anetra's mass moved off her throne. She went over to the frosted rose and touched her bejeweled heel to it. The rose shattered.

Sturgis realized now where he had heard those words "Zero-Kelvin." That was a temperature. Absolute zero degrees. Minus four-hundred something degrees Celsius!

Anetra smiled. Pinky came over to her. He had put on

160

a fiberglass glove, and he reached down for the shattered rose and picked up the sharp frozen shards of the flower and crushed them in his glove. The fine powder that was left he let sift onto the floor. "Now we will do the same to your wife. Unless you tell us what we want. And don't think you can lie. We have another device, courtesy of this beautiful base of operations that we have inherited. It is a lie detector of the most perfect sort. It is aimed at you right now — see that red dot in the wall? It will analyze your answers, and flash blue if you lie."

The colonel thought he might as well try and answered a few questions to stall. Each time he gave an answer, the light flashed blue.

Pinky frowned. "You are most uncooperative, and now we must render justice." He motioned to Pod 97. Sturgis expected that the robed lackey would go over to Robin with the hose-of-death. But no. Instead he left the room.

Pinky, in way of explanation, said, "The process of freezing is similar with roses and people. But we have to use a large chamber for a person. It is a slower death, and besides, I wish to keep Robin intact, to perhaps use her freeze-dried body as a decoration in our bedroom."

"Bastard," Sturgis gasped. Soon he saw Pod 97 returning with several other robed idiots. They wheeled into the throne room what looked like a decompression chamber — a steel-with-rivets chamber with a glass door.

"Place the colonel's wife inside the freeze-dry chamber," Pinky said.

As Robin was manhandled screaming into the chamber and the door sealed, the colonel struggled without success again to free himself from his chains.

Sturgis watched helplessly as Robin banged on the glass door and shouted — He could see her lips move, but not hear a sound.

"Begin the freeze-dry process," Anetra intoned. "Use

the slowest setting."

"Stop! I'll tell you everything," Sturgis shouted. And he meant it.

Pinky tut-tutted him. "Really, Colonel," Pinky said, "we don't need that information very badly, do we? The empress and I have this great big underground fortress full of high-tech devices. We have many soldiers as well. We can handle any attack, any eventuality, without your C.A.D.S. equipment. Keep your codes. Keep your information. It is *too late!*"

Sturgis moaned and cried out as he watched the frantic attempts of his wife to get out of the freeze-chamber. He watched in horror as over a period of about a half hour Robin pounded on the glass, an anguished expression on her turning-blue lips. And then Robin moved slower and slower, her eyelids covered with ice, her hair stiff like winter grass. Finally she was frozen in the position of banging on the glass. Frozen stiff.

Sturgis moaned and wept as Anetra and Pinky cackled in glee. The gauge stopped at minus four hundred sixty degrees.

"Now, take the chamber away, gently, Pods," Pinky ordered. "And keep her in one piece. I have an idea. I owe the Russians a gift. Premier Veloshnikov will be pleased to have Robin as a freeze-dried stuffed toy." He glared at Sturgis. "Colonel, you see, if the temperature in that chamber is very slowly raised over a period of months, she will lose all her body moisture. She will be as light as a feather. Freeze-drying is the simplest form of taxidermy, I have learned. Robin will live on as a fifty-pound stuffed toy. A couch-pillow for the Russians to toss around and play with."

Sturgis was beside himself in grief. The only consolation was that Robin probably had felt little pain. Freezing is one of the easier ways to die. He wondered whether he would be as lucky. And all of a sudden, he didn't care any more. What did anything matter now, with Robin dead? He no longer even thought about what Jeeters was or was not doing to destroy the fort. He just didn't give a flying fuck any more.

"Take Colonel Sturgis to the cells in area P," Pinky ordered. "Place the freeze-dry chamber in front of his cell. Let him look at her. Let him look at his wife from the cell. Sturgis, you can stare at Robin and shiver. You'll be stripped, Colonel. And the cold from the walls of her chamber near you will make you very uncomfortable. Then, let's see, what will it be? I should have something special arranged for you to endure. You will not get off as lightly as your wife! You and your men—particularly Billy Dixon, who tortured me (see C.A.D.S. #3) once, will have to endure much before you die.—Anetra, do you have any ideas on how he should die?"

"Well, honey, perhaps there should be some starving rats sent into his cell. Perhaps after a few days of starvation for the colonel. We can watch as he tries to fend them off. Who shall eat whom? Will the colonel eat the rats, or will he be eaten alive? It can be a contest. We can place bets."

"Sick. You're sick, Anetra." Sturgis said softly.

"That's what my cuddly-poops likes about me, Colonel."

"Yes," Pinky said. "She is as sick as I am!" Pinky snapped his fingers. "Take him away. Set up some cameras at his cell so we might observe Sturgis in his agony. Place a monitor in our bed chamber, so we may watch him tonight. I so tire of the video-tapes in the library. I long for live entertainment."

Chapter Twenty-three

The Reverend Jerry Jeff Jeeters had been shown every courtesy of the fort. First he was cleaned up and given new clothes—a shimmering golden robe of a "high" Disciple of Anetra's cult. When he was wined and dined, he had tried to look at ease, despite his intense desire to start poking around the fort on his own, and find tunnel 333. Maybe he could find some other way, a way for them to escape and not die.

The friendly mercenary officers and cultists who kept him company finally returned to other duties, and Jeeters thought that at last he could begin his work. Then, when he was alone for the first time and about to sneak into the labyrinth of tunnels to begin his desperate search, an honor guard came for him. He was taken to see the imperial couple—right after the colonel and the two women were removed.

When Jeeters was ushered into the throne room—which had the peculiar smell of dry ice and was unnaturally cold—Jeeters was immediately set upon for a favor by Pinky.

The fat menace spoke as soon as Jeeters had sat down in the easy chair that had been placed before the throne for his comfort. "Jeeters," Pinky said, "I want you to marry us. Anetra and I will be man and wife."

Jeeters responded with the words, "Er, I suppose I could. Yes. Surely. Er . . . when do you—"

"Right now," Anetra cut in. "It will be a small wedding; only our closest friends will be in attendance."

"N-Now?" Jeeters groaned inwardly. He had important work to do right now. He had to find tunnel 333. Sturgis had obliquely intimated—during their surrender—what he must do: Once he found the tunnel, Jeeters should sabotage the nuke-reactor, and put an end to this threat to the world. He didn't want to delay a moment longer. If America couldn't have the base, then no one would!

"Well, are you dumbstruck, Reverend? Don't you want to see us married? We are honorable people, Jeeters. We don't want to live in sin. Marry us."

"Yes . . . yes of course," Jeeters mumbled, "you're a lovely couple."

"Fine," Pinky snapped, "then we will have our wedding. Now. *Do it!*"

The reverend stammered, "Who—who will give away the bride?"

"Oh, you will attend to all of that!" Pinky snapped. "We have all our friends here. You can rehearse it all while we have a snack. Take as long as you want. Up to five minutes."

Jeeters looked around. "Your friends are here?" All the reverend saw were some gold-robed disciples and a few honor guards carrying deadly looking sten-guns.

"These *are* our friends," Pinky snapped, "and they are also our top officers and disciples." He was apparently irritated. "Aren't they good enough? They worship and serve us. What more proof of friendship can one have?"

"Of-of course," Jeeters stammered. He pulled out his pink mini-bible from the pouch pocket in his robe. It had been his good luck charm for years, maybe it would serve him well here too.

"Now do it," Pinky warned. "And I want this to be nice. I want you to make the ceremony sweet. I will hold this gun on you," the grumpy groom said, pulling a Luger from his belt. "You will make this ceremony lovely, or I will kill you, Jeeters."

"Ah, yes. Of course. Do you—er—have a religious preference?"

"Why do you ask," Anetra said, glaring.

"Er—I mean, what kind of wedding you want? What type of religious service—"

"A religious marriage?" Anetra laughed. "I am a goddess. I can't be married in the name of some lesser God! Surely you know that!"

"N-non religious, then," Jeeters countered. "Yes, of course. It can be done. Yes, I suppose that would be okay." Jeeters could see no way out of wasting time he so desperately needed, so he decided to rush, as requested.

"Okay," he said, taking a deep breath, "You, the disciple on the left—come over here and stand behind Pinky. Pinky, come stand here before me. Anetra, would you be so kind as to stand next to your groom. And you—the honor guard with the moustache—come stand next to Anetra."

When this was done, Jeeters opened the pink bible. "Dear friends, we have here in all splendor, the bride and groom, the honorable Pinky Ellis and Anetra. Dearly beloved," Jeeters intoned in his best friendly-yet-sincere-and-holy voice, "we are gathered here in the sight of—er—our friends and before—er—whoever or whatever runs the universe, if there is such a person or thing . . ."

"Get on with it," the fat groom said, placing his Luger up against the reverend's left temple, and staring down his plump nose.

"Do you Pinky Ellis, take—"

"*Emperor* Pinky Ellis," the groom corrected, cocking the Luger.

"Y-yes of course! Do you, *Emperor* Pinky Ellis, take this lovely woman, Goddess Anetra, to be your blushing bride?" The fat goddess smiled and Pinky moved the gun a few inches farther away from Jeeters's skull in response.

"—to be your lawfully wedded wife?"

"I do," the Emperor replied, jowls twitching in excitement.

"And do you, Anetra—er, what's your last name?"

"I have no last name. I'm a goddess!"

"Of course! Do you, Anetra, take this man to be your lawful wedded husband?"

"I do, oh, I do!"

"Then I pronounce you man and wife."

Pinky glared.

"I mean, I pronounce you *Emperor and Empress!* You may kiss."

They did. They osculated until Jerry thought he would retch. But at least the gun wasn't at his noggin. Finally they broke apart and Pinky, wiping saliva from his chins said, "Nice ceremony, Reverend."

"Perhaps you want me to—er—leave now," the reverend asked, closing the bible. "So you may be alone."

"Yes," Pinky gasped, "oh yes! Come to me, my sweet. Let us make love. Right here on the royal carpet!"

As the group of "friends" withdrew and walked down the corridor, along with the reverend, Jeeters heard the frantic love-words of the newly married couple. Anetra's voice was particularly loud: "Oh, yes, *there*. Yes . . . *Yes!* Faster and harder! That's it! Now! Faster and harder!"

Jeeters suppressed a barf and turned quickly down a corridor on his own, losing his companions. He had to find tunnel 333.

Jeeters still wore the golden robe of a high disciple of the Cult of the White Light. And though he passed

167

several guards at strategic points in the maze of tunnels, no one stopped him, or questioned him. With the golden robe on, it appeared that he had access to all the fort! The reverend previously had some doubts about destroying the fort — and himself and all his friends along with it, but now he had none. It would be worth dying to rid the world of that pair of perverted miscreants, never mind to prevent Pinky's Soviet allies from using Fort Collins. It would be a victory.

"I will do it, I will do it," Jeeters vowed between clenched teeth, as he took a right turn and went down a staircase. The numbers on the tunnel walls were rising. This was tunnel 331, and hopefully the next one would be 332. Soon he'd be in the heart of the beast, and could accomplish his death mission. He'd do as the colonel wanted: blow up the whole damned place.

Chapter Twenty-four

To the seagulls circling above the smooth green of the Atlantic Ocean, the first hints of something large beneath the surface brought alarm, then fear. The disturbance in the waves became massive, and as the shape beneath the waters took form, the seagulls wheeled away, sensing evil.

The immense menace soon surfaced, pushing aside a million gallons of water with no difficulty as it rose. It was a smooth dark thing: it looking like some primeval behemoth of ancient days. Perhaps the gulls perceived it to be a predatory sea-animal — an enormous hammerhead shark, or killer whale. Whatever it was, they knew it was something to stay away from.

The steadily moving black shape was not flesh and sinew, but metal. It was an undersea warship the size of a football field. It was a disk of death, an arsenal of Armageddon. This *thing* was a more vicious beast than anything natural that had ever roamed the world's deep waters. It was no common beast of prey, desiring food, fighting off its rivals. This was an *evil* that only the mind of man could conceive. This monster had nearly destroyed the world.

The three hundred meter long smooth blue-black metal shape parting the waves was the giant Soviet command submarine *Lenin*. The ultimate sea-power. It sounded like a living thing as it moved. There was a heartbeat in the metal beast, and a pulse, and breathing. But the heartbeat was the sound of a thousand pumps, and the pulse was from the million miles of circuitry, the breathing was the combined respirations of ten thousand humans. The crew was the elite of the technical arm of the Soviet Empire: Inside the *Lenin* were housed the best electronic countermeasures men, the best munitions handlers, missile trackers, torpedo tube operators. And there were women too. For lower duties. They were the most beautiful of all Soviet women, specially trained in the art of giving pleasure, selected for their skill at soothing the frayed nerves and tensed coiled bodies of the men in the *Lenin*.

These men of the *Lenin* never left the ship. Never in the past seven years, anyway. Not since the Final War commenced. And these men therefore needed to be relieved of their pent-up desires. Needed to be welcomed in the many small bedrooms inhabited by these temptresses.

The *Lenin* was the most formidable command-attack center that had ever been conceived. From the *Lenin* had come the Christmas Eve, 1997 orders to begin World War Three. From the *Lenin* had come the insidious voice of mega-death that commanded Soviet forces worldwide to launch their surprise attack, right in the middle of a world peace conference.

The voice of death within the *Lenin* was deep in timber, filled with cunning and hate. It was the voice of the man called Supreme Marshal Mikael Veloshnikov. A man to be feared. A man supposedly invincible.

And yet . . . things had gone wrong. The man-to-be-feared was himself afraid this day. For the U.S. was still fighting back. Mostly the resistance was a ragtag opposition that would eventually be crushed. But there was a greater threat to Soviet hegemony: The C.A.D.S. troopers. That small unit of metal-clad men with god-like powers of destruction scared Veloshnikov. The C.A.D.S. unit, America's high-tech answer to the Soviet invasion force, a band of warriors that had sent the Soviet Union reeling.

That legendary counter force was very much on the mind of the scar-faced man in crisp black uniform who now sat alone in the dimness and cool of the "Nautilus Room" at the foremost bow of the massive submarine. This heavy-eyebrowed gaunt man scowled out at the passing undersea world beyond the foot thick window without paying it attention. Fantastic creatures of the sea darted this way and that to avoid the vessel, but he paid them no heed. Supreme Marshal Veloshnikov was lost in his thoughts. Thoughts of how to finish off the United States and rule the world. And no matter how long or hard he thought, the only way he could find to win was to kill off the C.A.D.S. troopers.

This one restive lonely man had spent the past six hours in the "Nautilus Room" poring over the sketchy reports from Moscow. Reports dealing with the power struggle there. Reports on how his force was doing against the multitude of other factions trying to seize control of the Kremlin in the wake of the devastation that the C.A.D.S. men had wrought there. His eyes had finally started to hurt. So the supreme marshal turned out the lights and just stared at the water. And thought about his chances to win the whole world. Could he actually pull of the feat that Alexander the Great, Caesar, Hitler, Mao had failed to accomplish? Yes. If things went well, Veloshnikov could take it all. Rule the whole world.

The reports from Moscow were encouraging. There were more and more confirmations every hour: His faction was wiping out the last bits of resistance. Already most commanders in the field, most officers in the various conquered territories, were admitting that Veloshnikov was the winner.

The last report Veloshnikov had received was the best. The American Occupation force's chief, Merkerov, had declared for Veloshnikov. He had stated that his acceptance would have been broadcast sooner, were it not for the sabotage of the large transmitter tower in Hartsdale, South Carolina. It seemed that the marshal's suspicions about Reverend Jeeters, alleged champion of the Soviet cause, had proven correct. The reverend had been a double agent, feeding information to the renegade Americans—somehow—during his televised Bible Hour broadcasts. Now those renegades had snatched Jeeters from the descending hand of Soviet justice, just a few minutes before the reverend was to be arrested. And the renegades had destroyed the broadcast tower as part of their rescue.

Well, Veloshnikov thought, that resistance was the minor problem now. What could a few ragtag renegades and a bible thumper do to harm the great Soviet Empire? It was the C.A.D.S. force that was the real worry. Allegedly, they had been dealt with. Reports said the C.A.D.S. unit had been wiped out by a germ-laden missile and follow up nuke-missile aimed at their base.

But Veloshnikov was not so sure. He wanted to see bodies. Especially the C.A.D.S. commander's body. Sturgis was very tricky.

He sighed. Perhaps he was too worried. After all, with Merkerov's acknowledgment of his position as the new Premier, that meant Veloshnikov was the most powerful man who had ever lived. Now everyone would fall into line! If the C.A.D.S. unit was still functioning, he would do what the last premier had failed to do: Bend every resource to their destruction.

The supreme marshal tried to relax. He leaned back with his hands behind his head in the comfortable swivel chair and stared at the panoply of sea-life before the window. A large sucker fish came along, and it stuck itself to the glass. It was hanging on the window, blocking his view. How *dare* it!

A leer crossed the supreme marshal's scarred face. He could have some fun now. Why not? Amusements were hard to come by for the jaded leader. Veloshnikov pressed the electric charge button that sent a million volts of electricity into the reinforced windowglass.

Instantly the huge sucker fish jerked in a spasm of pain and detached from the glass. It slowly glided away, dead as a doornail. "Goodbye, my enemies, goodbye," the supreme marshal muttered. If only he could be sure that Colonel Sturgis and the C.A.D.S. troopers had likewise been eliminated. Veloshnikov tried to picture the American troopers being hit by the nuke missile. Tried to picture them gasping for breath when the Americans were surprised by the sudden explosion of a bomb in the midst of their base. Tried to imagine the American colonel sitting bolt-upright in his bed, reaching for his throat, trying to breath. Perhaps the American officer had survived the germ-attack, safe in his C.A.D.S. suit. Had he been hit by the follow up nuke-missile? Had Sturgis died inside the overheated metal suit? Had he died jerking in spasms when the radiation bore through his shields of titanium steel? Had he been reduced to a few random atoms wafting on the radioactive breeze of the western U.S.?

The latest reports had confirmed that the secret American base at White Sands had been destroyed. There was supposedly nothing to worry about any more. But he had to be sure! He had a gut feeling that something had gone wrong and that Colonel Sturgis was *alive.*

There was a knock at the metal door, a low booming noise that was very irritating. Veloshnikov decided that he would have that door better insulated.

"Come in," he said angrily, and swiveled his chair to face the portal as it opened.

"Sir," the man silhouetted in the light of the corridor gasped, "there is a radio report that has just been received: Our ally Pinky Ellis and his mercenaries have captured Fort Collins, the long sought for underground U.S. base. They have the President of the United States and Colonel Sturgis of the C.A.D.S. unit in custody there."

Veloshnikov stood up and strode to the messenger and he snapped the report from the young man's sweaty fingers. "I will read this myself," he said.

Veloshnikov brought the report over to his mahogany desk and switched on the light. As he read it, the report got better and better. Robin Adler, Sturgis's wife, had been captured along with the colonel. That was good. The Russians had been made chumps of to the world when Sturgis had rescued his wife from the Kremlin torture chamber. Now, the world would know that the rescue had been cancelled.

What? The supreme marshal read the next lines again and again. Pinky had Robin quick-frozen! What? What kind of hare-brained idea was that? Pinky was an idiot! Veloshnikov cursed aloud. That fat American idiot really should have saved her. Veloshnikov would have liked to interrogate her. Oh well, he supposed Ellis deserved his fun. He had been very useful to the Soviet cause. It was kind of a funny thing to do!

Veloshnikov quickly scanned the last several pages of the communique. There was a request that he come and visit Fort Collins, and some details of the celebration that Ellis planned for his arrival.

"Yes," he said, handing the report back to the lackey. "I will go to Fort Collins! Send out a dispatch to that effect at once. Tell Pinky Ellis that I will be arriving in—" he glanced at his 34 jewel watch. "Six hours."

"Isn't that a bit tight, sir?" the lackey asked.

"You are not paid to question orders!" Veloshnikov snapped. Then, as the orderly paled, the marshal smiled. "But you are correct. Make that seven hours."

The man saluted and left. Veloshnikov spent a few minutes staring out at the waters parting before the bow. He had known that Sturgis was alive, and now it had been confirmed. Confirmed in the most salutory way! He must get to the fabled Fort Collins as fast as possible and take over from this Pinky Ellis. From what Veloshnikov knew of that fort, it could be the key power base in the world. A fit post-nuclear capital. And once he secured the fort, there would be no need to coddle this Ellis character any more.

Veloshnikov leaned over and snapped the intercom switch. "Admiral Vestok! Immediately assemble an attack commando unit — to be disguised as a large contingent of honor guards — for my visit to this American Fort Collins. Each man should be the best. I want killers who can fight with their hands and feet if no weapons are available. I want the best."

"How many men?" the admiral queried.

"About fifty. Any more will arouse suspicion. I want some highly trained technicians along also. A dozen men expert at unravelling the mysteries of American technology. We have to learn all about the capabilities of that fort, once we take over. Can you do this in time for my departure?"

"Sir," came the reply, "the Spetznaz commandos on board have fifty men who meet your requirements. As for the technicians, the nearest group of a dozen specialists is at Polar Station Zasta. That's four hours away from our position."

"Good enough! Have them take off immediately for Fort Collins. Send the technicians the co-ordinates. I and the commandos will meet them at the fort."

"It will be done immediately, sir."

"Admiral Vestok, there is one more thing. I have admired your handling of the crew and your help in several past endeavors. While I am gone, you will be in charge here. And when the fort is secured, there will be a Vice-Premiership position for you. You will be second in command of the world."

After the sound of air being sucked in, the admiral replied, "You are most kind, excellency. But won't the Supreme Soviet Congress, when it is formed once more, have to confirm my appointment?"

"A mere formality. From now on, I make *all* the decisions." The marshal frowned, "You understand, Admiral, don't you?"

"Yes sir! Thank you sir for your confidence."

Veloshnikov cut off the intercom. He smiled. Vestok had not tried to dissuade him from risking his life in the seizure of Fort Collins. The admiral was probably thinking that Veloshnikov would be killed. The admiral probably *hoped* that Veloshnikov would be killed.

The stakes were high. Many men wished to have the ultimate power, and not be second. But few would take the risks necessary to accomplish that. Veloshnikov was going to take that risk, and he wasn't going to die. He was going to deliver a master stroke, and with that one calculated move, he would be in a position to rule everything.

Within a few hours the submarine's steel flight-deck doors whirred open and out came the twin-engine Stol flyer. It was a nuclear powered jet with a two-man crew. And room for one passenger: The supreme marshal himself.

Dressed in a black flight suit and carrying an attache

case, Veloshnikov carefully strode across the half-awash deck and got on board the jet. The canopy closed. He strapped himself in and looked up into the blue sky. He saw the seven troop-carrying jets that would accompany his jet to Fort Collins were already launched and high up. Good. Veloshnikov put his helmet on and said, "Take off."

The roar of the jet engines and the sudden intense acceleration were not as disturbing as the jerk of the catapult-assisted takeoff boost. The marshal was thrown back in the cushioned seat like he had been shoved by a giant hand. For a second he thought he would black out.

But then the acceleration eased, and the plane banked. The marshal looked back down at the submarine. The *Lenin* was already just a small bluish disk in the vast ocean. It was drooping down below the waters. Then the plane levelled off and Veloshnikov stared straight ahead. He watched the warm midday sun bend and diffract on the canopy, creating rainbows in the plastic.

He closed his eyes. He would get a few hours sleep. He needed rest if he was to pull off this deception. He needed to be at his peak if he wanted to take over the American fort with just fifty men!

Chapter Twenty-five

As Supreme Marshal Veloshnikov's ramjet flashed over the waters of the Atlantic heading toward them, Pinky and Anetra made frantic preparations. The pair of flabby ultimate-rulers were doing their level best to prepare for his visit. They wanted so much to impress the supreme marshal, especially Pinky. For years Pinky had admired the Russian. Pinky knew that Veloshnikov was the key man in the vast — and mostly successful — war against the Free World. What a good job Veloshnikov had done in decimating two-thirds of the planet! To Pinky, the originator of that war was a man to be admired for his daring and vision. No one had ever destroyed as much in so short a time!

If it were not for the great war, Pinky knew that he would never have been in the enviable position he now enjoyed. Pinky Ellis would have been a mere common, ordinary, run-of-the-mill Philadelphia millionaire, hounded by lawsuits. Before the nuking, Pinky had been trapped in a world that didn't respect him. He had been trapped in a web of complicated government restrictions, regulations that hamstrung his business operations. Consumer and public interest groups had nearly shut down Pinky's profitable synthofood distribution plant, and nosey congressmen and reporters had threatened to expose cost overruns and design problems in Pinky's many Defense Department contracts.

Besides, he hadn't been having much fun before the war either. Yes, he owed Veloshnikov a lot. Ever since the bombs had dropped, Pinky had a ball — with the exception of a few times — like the time he had been buried alive in an anthill. Since the war began, it had been one big party! No more tax and regulation worries, no women problems, no limits to Pinky's whim to maim and torture and control! And he owed it all to Veloshnikov.

Pinky stood now and looked down over the work progressing on the main hall of the fort-complex. The hundred-foot-wide, half mile long main underground corridor was lined with endless machines — metal life support and power equipment. Real Dullsville. But Pinky and his beautiful consultant Empress Anetra had decided to cover the boring machines over with brightly colored bunting. Ribbons and flags made of silk fabric or crepe paper now made the scene an avenue of festivity. They had used all the decorations they could find. Whatever the fort's storehouse contained; and that was a lot.

There had been found a whole room full of the decorative material. This fort was full of surprises. It was big, real big. Pinky still really had no idea exactly how big. The fort was meant, he knew, as a last refuge for the elite of America, a self-contained world. An impregnable base. But those elite had been surprised by the suddenness of the Soviet attack, so they had never made it into Fort Collins. Judging from the amount of material suitable for parades and parties, the fort's makers probably had planned many happy celebrations here, while the world burned. And now Pinky and his beautiful bride were the beneficiary of all that fine decoration. And they would share their luck with the Russian strongman!

The fat emperor smiled and he held Anetra close to him. Pinky couldn't quite get his meaty arm around the empress's waist, but halfway would do. "Isn't the bunting lovely," he said, "I especially like the red streamers, and those pictures of Stalin. Where on earth did you find pictures of Stalin, dear?"

"Oh," the empress replied, "My disciples found several large pictures of Teddy Roosevelt. I had some of my more artistic cultists alter his picture a bit, and *voila!* Stalin!"

"Brilliant, my dear, simply brilliant!"

"Yes, it was. But it was your brilliant idea, Pinky, to have all that pink bunting around the reception stage. It is so compatible with the red!"

"Isn't it a bit dim in here, my dear?" Pinky worried.

She smiled, and leaned over and flicked a switch on the intercom panel. Her voice boomed out down the long corridor. "Turn on the lightshow, Pod 37."

Far down the corridor, a stone-eyed disciple with a yellow robe bent to his knees in obedience and then turned and jammed two plugs together. Instantly the effect appeared and it was nearly blinding. All along the balconies on both sides of the underground esplanade laser lights shot out. They moved around like searchlights, danced and reflected off the many mirror covered balls strung about on the ceiling. "How's that," she boasted. "Isn't it just like a disco?"

"Pretty," Pinky said, somewhat taken aback. "But — you don't think Veloshnikov will think it a bit too disco-ish?"

"Are you saying it's tacky? Hmmmph! Glitter is *never* tacky, Pinky, my husband."

Pinky dropped the subject. "By the way, darling," he said, "I haven't see the reverend around — have you? I'd like him to see this."

"You're right," Anetra replied, "We should send for Jeeters." She got on the intercom and ordered, "Everyone that's not busy on decorating! Stop standing around and find Reverend Jeeters. Does anyone know where he is?"

There was a lot of scurrying around but no reply came to her question. Pinky frowned, and he got on the loudspeaker, "All first rank soldiers of my army will search for Reverend Jeeters. Start with the hydroponic-garden area. I want the reverend to stand beside us and greet the supreme marshal, who will be arriving in about—" Pinky glanced at his Rolex, "—about twenty minutes. My God, get that red carpet rolled out! We haven't much time! Hurry it up!"

Pod 8 pulled Pod 17 into a dark corner between two immense hydraulic pumps.

"What are you doing?" Pod 17 asked, trying to pull away.

"Shhhh! This is top secret," Pod 8 said. "We have to talk. There are those among us—I hope you are one—who do not like this marriage that our glorious goddess has undergone."

"Yes," Pod 17 said glumly. "I agree that it is not a fitting marriage. But our goddess has chosen, and we must acquiesce."

Pod 8 made a scoffing noise and said, "She has been influenced by some occult power, by some evil force of the man she married. We should not be ruled by him. This is an abomination. Here," Pod 8 added, "have some of the supreme white powder. Sniff it and you will understand that I am right when I say we must change this awful situation."

Pod 17's large cornflower-blue eyes widened in amazement. "But—but only the goddess's official distributors, the senior Pods, can distribute the holy powder!" Despite this pronouncement, Pod 17 eagerly took the small vial of addictive euphoria-mixture offered him and placed it against his flared nostrils and sniffed.

"We have changed all that," said Pod 8, as Pod 17's big

blues rolled in pleasure. "Here, have a little more powder. This time, swallow it! You look a bit strung out. We all are strung out. Since the marriage, the amount of joy-powder we have all been given has been cut drastically. So some of us broke open the supply and we're helping ourselves. We should feel good, not bad. Because the powder is being distributed to Pinky's men now, we don't have enough for ourselves. And it will quickly run out. Then what would we do?"

"I can't agree more," Pod 17 said, his eyes rolling up into his forehead as he swallowed the ecstasy-mix.

"It is good that you understand. We can have *all* the white powder, we can have our goddess back. But only if we act boldly."

"What do we do?"

Pod 8's eyes narrowed. "Pinky must die during the celebrations. We have devised a plan. Those decorative lasers, focused all together, can be deadly. We will aim all the lasers directly at Pinky, when he stands up on the welcoming stage."

"But their concentrated power will harm our goddess. She will be standing next to Pinky."

"No, we will aim carefully, Pod 17. And then, things will be as before. We can get back to our corn-farming on the surface. Back to our idyllic life."

"Back to sunny paradise," Pod 17 said with joy in his words.

"Yes! It is gloomy down here underground. We are the children of the New Eden, and we belong upstairs."

"Children of the New Eden," Pod 17 repeated, chewing over the words and liking the taste. "Yes I agree." He looked hungrily at the other Anetra disciple. "Er, may I have some more?"

"Most certainly."

* * *

Down in the main fuse room of the fortress, several of Pinky's men gathered around a table playing cards were discussing the situation as well.

"I don't like the damned cultists," snarled Levinsky, Pinky's chief aide. "Anetra is a nut case, and her disciples are a bunch of syncophantic shitfaces." He wiped a sheen of sweat from his bald pate. "The fat woman will ruin our boss; there will be no more adventure, no more raping and pillaging out there in the real world. This marriage *sucks*."

Gromley, the player with a hook for a left hand, agreed. "I don't like this whole thing neither. They make me nervous with their stupid grins. Why do we need the cultists now anyway? There would be more for us if they died."

"Well, they could be useful in running this fort," the third of the poker players said, looking a bit nervous for contradicting the others. "It's very big, you know."

"Bah," Levinsky retorted, tossing another potato chip into his mouth and crunching it. "I say we can do without them. This whole place is fully automated. These cultist allies of ours could be dangerous. And besides, Pinky will favor them over us! That woman has him wrapped around her fat finger! She softened the boss. And softness in this world means death."

"Well, what do we do?" Gromley asked, throwing down his hand. "What *can* we do?"

Levinsky leaned forward over the cards and spoke very slowly and in a low voice. "I say we figure some way to eliminate the fat broad and her disciples." The assistant-chief reached for his holster and put his .45 down on the table. "I favor the direct approach. Kill this Anetra. Once she's dead, the boss will find no use for those blithering cultists. He'll come back to his senses."

"No," Gromley gasped. "Pinky won't like it."

"Stupid," Levinsky sneered, "It will be like the Kennedy thing. We'll set up a patsy—one of Anetra's senior Pods. We'll do it the same way—have several guys in different positions, a crossfire. One of our men is bound to hit her. We'll leave one of her senior Pods holding a rifle."

"Like Oswald," the third man laughed. He laughed so hard that he fell off his chair. Which set Levinsky to laughing too.

"Yeah, I suppose it might be possible," Gromley said, nodding his head. "But we can't hit the boss. We need him! Even if Pinky is cruel, he always knows what to do. We've survived because of him all these years."

"It's settled then," Levinsky said, confidently. "Now here's my plan . . ."

After his commandos disguised as gold-helmeted honor guards had landed and debarked from their transport jets near the fort's entrance, Veloshnikov's jet settled down on the flat desert. The supreme marshal climbed down from his seat and looked at the rows of strange robed men and the khaki-clad mercenaries that were arrayed before him. There was a blare of trumpets, an off-key fanfare for his arrival.

A pair of the khaki-clad mercenaries came to him and saluted. They said they were honored to escort him to see Emperor Pinky and Empress Anetra.

With a raised eyebrow as his only response to the ridiculous titles, Veloshnikov nodded. He let himself be led down a ramp, with his fifty men following closely behind. He soon entered an air-conditioned maze of tunnels, and the escort pair chose the largest one to walk down. The taller one told Veloshnikov that he would soon be in the main area of the fort. They passed vast pumping stations, air purifying areas, hydroponics rooms full of growing plants in mineral-rich water. Then the Soviet leader saw some of the parked Bandersnatch air-tanks, and the row upon row of ground vehicles, some with the triangle symbol meaning nuclear-powered. My God, what a place! What power it held!

Even before they reached the main area, the supreme marshal was more than just impressed. It was vast, so vast. He smiled when his escort pointed out the door to an area called "S.A. testing chamber." The talkative escort said that Pinky and his men didn't yet know the intended use for the modules inside that chamber. But, the man said, Pinky had used one of the modules to quick-freeze a prisoner.

Veloshnikov smiled obsequiously. But inside his heart pounded wildly. S.A.! He knew that meant Suspended Animation, one of America's last and greatest endeavors! There had been rumors that the Americans were well on their way to perfecting S.A. before the Great War. That idiot Pinky actually didn't understand what S.A. signified. S.A. was a way to sleep your way into the next century!

This whole place and all its wonders was definitely wasted on these jerks, Veloshnikov realized. They didn't understand at all what they had in Fort Collins! It wasn't just a military fort, it was a vast habitat, a self-contained world for long term post-nuke survival.

And soon it would be his.

Chapter Twenty-Six

Pinky and Anetra sat in the dark giggling like school-children. They were waiting on the esplanade's balcony for Veloshnikov to step into the vast darkened space, and then they would spring their surprise on him. The pair had been monitoring the supreme marshal's progress through the fort and now they knew that he was less than fifty yards from their great welcoming party.

"All right," Pinky whispered over the mike, "Remember to hit the switch for the laser light show when I give the word. And you in the Pod orchestra — don't forget, I want the Soviet national anthem played with verve! Make those tubas loud. Make it sound like John Philip Sousa is here! And cut in early with the pipe-organs and Tibetan trumpets. — You on the ceiling scaffold: Once the first note is hit and the lights come on, drop the balloons. Wait until I yell 'surprise.' "

"Just wait," Anetra said, cuddling up to her lover in the dark, "until he sees this! Will our guest love it, darling? Will he appreciate it?" She searched Pinky's left ear with her tongue and found it full of earwax.

"Of course he'll love it," Pinky moaned. "The Russians are all crazy about ceremony."

"Right this way, sir," said the taller man escorting the marshal. "Please go down that ramp."

"But there are no lights on in there," Veloshnikov hesitated.

"They come on by electric eye," Pinky's man said. "Don't worry."

Veloshnikov said, "I *never* worry." He snapped his fingers and ten of his elite commandos came forward and formed a phalanx around him. "Lead on," Veloshnikov said. "I'm sure you won't mind if I have my honor guard enter with me."

The commandos moved forward with the supreme marshal, resplendent in their black and silver trim uniforms and many medals. Perhaps Pinky's men didn't notice how fit the Russian honor guards were beneath their silly ceremonial uniforms. They were all tall and muscular. And they were all killers. They silently acknowledged the wave of their leader's hand and formed up into a defensive wedge as he descended the ramp toward the darkness.

Veloshnikov, as he stared at the blackness before him, became a little nervous. Could there be some sort of trap ahead? No, that idiot traitor Ellis, according to Intel, worshipped the ground that the supreme marshal walked upon. Besides, the commandos could handle anything with their white painted ceremonial rifles. After all, the rifles were really high-velocity action smg's loaded with explosive bullets. And the Russian honor guards' decorative 'wooden' bullets on their belts were actually mini-missiles. If he was separated from his men, the tiny mike implanted in his cheek gave him instant communications with his soldiers through their helmet speakers. He was ready for anything.

The supreme marshal took a step into the darkness. Suddenly the lights came on, as he had been promised. But *what lights!* His eyeballs were nearly blasted from their sockets as a million high-intensity lasers shot out across the vast hallway. His ears were assailed with the cacophony of hundreds of amplified musical instruments, blaring out a rendition of the Soviet *Internationale*.

Veloshnikov sank to his knees in shock as his troops leveled their guns in all directions and waited for his order to fire. But just as he was about to scream out orders to kill, a pair of voices screamed out "Surprise! Surprise!" And as the Russian maximum-leader looked up, he saw the two jewel-robed possessors of those twin voices step forward on a balcony high overhead. He recognized Pinky, but who the hell was the tubby broad with him?

And from all sides of the mile-long brilliantly lit corridor, men in white robes and soldiers in dull khaki stepped forward and yelled, "Welcome, Comrade!" Balloons fell from nets attached to the ceiling, the laser spotlights spun and reflected off many crystal balls spinning in the air.

And there were banners and streamers, some with the likeness of Stalin on them. As Veloshnikov's jaw stayed open in awe, the music changed from the Soviet anthem to a rendition of 'Moscow Girls Knock Me Out,' and it was not a bit lower in volume. My God, he realized, it was a welcoming celebration, not an attack. Veloshnikov stood up, and brushed off his knees and smiled and waved. His men, seeing him compose himself, lowered their deadly assault weapons and stood at attention, as overwhelmed as he was. The balcony where Pinky and his female companion stood now began to slowly descend on some sort of hydraulic drive.

Soon the pair of bejeweled maniacs were at Veloshnikov's level and they stepped forward. Pinky shook his hand. "How do you like the welcome?" Pinky asked.

The marshal hated the welcome, but he smiled and said, "Nice, real nice." Veloshnikov hoped that the sour feeling he had didn't show. He was anxious to have the ridiculous welcoming ceremony end, and get his men in position to eliminate this jowled lunatic and his plump female friend, and all their lunatic flock. "As much as I'd like to hear more of your glorious band," Veloshnikov shouted in perfect English, "Shouldn't we abbreviate the ceremonies a bit? There are many things to discuss. Your medal, for instance, Pinky."

"My medal?" Pinky smiled. "Yes, of course. But first I'd like you to meet my new bride, the Empress Anetra of Atlantis."

"Charmed," the Russian leader said in his best oily voice and kissed her plump left hand. She giggled. "Oh, I'm so glad you like our welcome!" She started shedding tears of joy, and gushed, "Pinky and I have worked so hard to make it the *best.*"

Veloshnikov nodded. "Simply unbelievable, let me assure you, your Majesty." He couldn't wait to have this pair of loonies shot. His eardrums and eyes would never be the same.

The Anetra cultists who were part of the assassination plot against Pinky were hidden among the piles of streamers and posters along the side of the great underground concourse. They were ready to shoot now; their sniper rifles were inside their robes, ready to be aimed at Pinky. But Pod Number 8 hesitated to give the signal. Goddess Anetra was standing too close to their target.

Ironically, standing just feet away from the seven men in robes about to cut down Pinky were six of the mercenary assassins, bent on killing Anetra. Levinsky was supposed to signal them when to shoot. He cursed as his boss Pinky Ellis moved even closer to their intended target. Levinsky wanted to have his men fire before the ceremony was over, before Anetra went back to her

189

secure quarters. But she wouldn't move an inch from the boss!

"I have a speech prepared," Pinky said. He signaled the Pod orchestra to ease up a bit.

"No time, I'm afraid," Veloshnikov countered, glancing at his watch. "The pressure of power makes all of us forsake even the most wonderful pleasures of life, don't you agree? Alas, the affairs of state must take precedent over those words I so long to hear. Might I suggest that we three confer on important matters, and that while we speak, your men show my men around the fortress?"

"Of course," Anetra said, still charmed by the Russian's hand-kissing gesture. "Let's all go up to the throne room and talk." Anetra, gathering the train of her blue-bejeweled gown, led the way. Veloshnikov muttered under his breath into his cheek-implanted mike. "Men, let the fools show you the whole place. Then spread out and secure the fort."

Those were orders for all but ten of them, who would come with Veloshnikov wherever he went. The Russian followed the Emperor and Empress.

Levinsky had been about to give the order to shoot. So had Pod 8. But to all the assassins' chagrin, the "ultimate couple" now departed with the Russian, clinging closely to one another as they left the podium. By the time the two opposing teams of assassins could again take a bead, the stage was empty.

As the royal couple and the Russian — together with ten of the Soviet commandos and a contingent of the royal guards — descended in a private elevator, Pinky said, "First, before we speak, we will have a snack. How about pheasant tongues, and some caviar, Supreme

Marshal? The freezers in this fort are well stocked with all sorts of delicacies. While you eat, you will have the opportunity to read the printed copy of our welcoming speeches. I don't want you to miss anything."

"How kind," Veloshnikov frowned.

Chapter Twenty-seven

Colonel Sturgis huddled in a corner of his cell, shivering naked. It seemed like a long time since they had brought him here and set up the capsule with his frozen wife inside it right in front of the cell bars. He didn't know if it had been just hours or a day that had passed since then. They set up the monitoring cameras, and then left him alone to stare at Robin, her face frozen in anguish. Left him to contemplate the stupidity of his idea of surrendering. If only he could undo that decision and die out there fighting like a man.

Pinky and Anetra's men had also set up a sort of rat-ramp leading into his cell. A clear plastic tube a foot wide filled with rats waiting in line to move. But they hadn't sent the starving rats into his cell yet. The door to the rat-chute stayed closed. His captors were probably just waiting for him to starve and freeze a little more before adding the final torture of tearing teeth and claws. Letting him wait for his end, making Sturgis suffer in the expectation of the horror.

Rats! Sturgis never thought they would be the instrument of his end. It would be awful. And with Robin staring at him from behind the frosty glass of the freeze-chamber, it would be worse. He hadn't looked at Robin at first, but then he finally did. And he felt the rebuke in her solid-ice brown eyes. Yet he stared and stared at her. He wanted to use Robin's death, wanted to let her frozen anguish be his incentive to turn the tables somehow on Pinky and Anetra. And Robin in death gave him all the anger and hatred for the "supreme couple" that any man could have.

But he still hadn't found a way to take revenge.

She was dead; he knew that. And yet — and yet Robin seemed alive. Why did he feel some hope? What madness was this?

He jumped up and down, breathing out clouds of cold air. Pretty soon now his captors wouldn't have the luxury of watching him get eaten alive by rats. He'd be long dead from exposure.

The speaker in the wall clicked and a voice came booming into the cell. "Sorry for the delay, Sturgis," Pinky said, "But it wasn't avoidable. You see, we got married. And then we had a visitor. We're entertaining him now. We've been all watching you jumping around. What do you think of that?"

"Can slime slugs marry in this state?" was Sturgis's only reply.

"Very funny. We'll see how funny you are soon, won't we dear?"

Sturgis heard Anetra's wild cackle.

"Soon, Sturgis," Pinky continued, "we will keep our promise to you. We will see what kind of a fight a naked man can put up against a thousand starving rats."

The colonel said nothing. He didn't even look up at the camera. He turned his back.

Pinky was not to be discouraged: "You know, Colonel, what we're doing right now? We are eating caviar with our guest. And do you know who he is?"

"Couldn't care less," Sturgis mumbled. But he was curious.

"Our guest is Supreme Marshal Veloshnikov, new

193

leader of the Soviet Empire, Colonel," Pinky boasted. "See how important we have become? He's here with us, in the throne room, watching you freeze. The marshal wanted to see you, wanted to watch you suffer a bit while he snacks on Beluga and drinks his cappuccino."

"Get stuffed, all of you," Sturgis huffed. But he was intrigued. Was Veloshnikov really in the fort? Sturgis smiled. If so, so much the better. Pinky made no mention of Jeeters. Jeeters might be roaming free, on his mission of destruction. If the reverend succeeded, the Russian madman would be blown up along with them all when the nuke reactor overloaded. Suddenly the colonel felt almost cheery! Who could ask for anything more? He just hoped the place would blow before the rats came at him!

"You are boring us, Colonel," a new voice spoke out. And Sturgis recognized the harsh tones of Veloshnikov! So the Russian torturer was here!

"Perhaps you will be less boring with some friends in the cell with you, Colonel," the Red butcher intoned.

The speaked clicked off and then there was a metallic clang. The colonel sucked in a deep breath as he saw that the plastic tubing that held the rats had opened. And coming forth like a medieval plague were the rats.

They were big fuckers! They were screeching, biting one another in an attempt to claim all the spoils of the feast. The rats each wanted to reach their naked human prey first.

Sturgis backed off, silently imploring, "Come on, Jeeters, do your thing!" What the hell could he fend them off with? It looked like he wasn't going to be around to witness the destruction of the fort, if it happened.

Then the door to the rat-tube closed shut again. Only twelve rats had made it into the cell. Just a dozen, this time. Maybe he could stomp them out, or smother them with his body. He'd get a few bites, but survive. Yeah,

194

and then another dozen rats would come in and then another. Naked, he was an easy victim. If he was in the C.A.D.S. suit, this would be child's play. But he wasn't. Sturgis lamented ever leaving his air-conditioned fighting machine. If he could only call his suit, like Roy Rogers called his horse Trigger in all those old western videodisks . . .

Sturgis kicked out at the forward-most rat just as he realized that his last thought had been *brilliant*. Theoretically at least, he could call his suit. His suit's name was Zeus and Martel had shown Sturgis back in the test cave at White Sands how it could respond to a voice. Maybe if Zeus could hear him, it would come now.

Yeah. That was the problem. If it could hear him. Where was the suit stored? Was it even in one piece?

No matter, Sturgis muttered, as he stomped a set of advancing rats into bones and bloody meat. He could try!

He finished off one after another of the rats, using kicks and fist-blows. It was a show for Pinky, his bride and the Soviet leader. They cheered or razzed him. But when he was finished, he changed the show. He got down on his knees and pretended to pray. "Oh Great Zeus, God of all," Sturgis prayed aloud, "Come to me. Come to your humble servant, come to Dean Sturgis! Save me!"

Hysterical laughter erupted from the speaker. Pinky and his guest and Anetra were howling in derision. "He prays to ancient gods!" Veloshnikov guffawed. "Can you believe it? He must be mad."

Sturgis kept shouting his "prayer," but he had little hope of the suit "hearing" him.

Then a remarkable bit of luck happened: Pinky had an idea that changed the colonel's luck: "Perhaps," the fat man said, "all the fort should hear this bold leader's whining plea to the gods. Perhaps his fellow captives should hear this begging!"

Sturgis kept praying. "Zeus, oh Zeus, come to me! Protect me!"

"Good idea," Veloshnikov said, chuckling. "Pinky, can you pipe it into the fort's P.A. system?"

"Can do," Pinky said, belly-laughing.

Sturgis remained on his knees, and he started shouting out all the names of the various suits. It was easy to remember the names! They were all named after ancient Greek and Indian gods. Holding the palms of his hands together, the colonel called out, "Oh, Siva, Oh Vishnu and Aphrodite, blessed Kali and Buddha; wondrous Krishna and Pan, help me! Go help your beloved C.A.D.S. troopers in their hour of need. Do it now!"

"Silly prayers," Veloshnikov complained, "I had more respect for Sturgis once. Now he is a simpering fool. I'm disgusted."

"Great Indra, great Athena, come to our rescue. Now!" Sturgis continued, hearing his voice amplified throughout the fortress, bouncing and echoing off every wall of the vast fortress.

"Shut it off," Veloshnikov said, "and send in some more rats!"

"Great Zeus, get off your butt and come to me!" Sturgis screamed. "Come to papa now, and save me!"

And just as the amp-system that had been broadcasting the colonel's words went dead all over the fort, the C.A.D.S. suits began responding in their storeroom. Zeus's onboard computer was programmed to hear and to interpret the commands of Dean Sturgis and now moved to do just that. Zeus's computer commanded that all systems in the armor-device become active and that they follow its marching orders.

The C.A.D.S. suits were all in one piece. They had been forgotten for the moment, and they were lined up hung on hooks in a storeroom for later perusal. But now the empty suits moved. They reached up their metal arms and lifted themselves off the hooks. They jumped down and stood up and started to walk like staggering drunks toward the metal doors. The first suit to move, Zeus, tore the door off its hinges, and then Kali and Krishna, and all the other suits followed the leader-suit down the hallway.

The mercenary technicians that were eating thawed out pastrami sandwiches in a nearby snack-bar turned when they heard the heavy footsteps and reached for their sidearms. But when they saw who—or rather *what*—was approaching, they scattered in horror, spilling their meals and their coffee and tea on the tile floor.

But the hapless technicians didn't get far. There was only one way in and out of the snack-bar. So, as they tried to make it past the animated C.A.D.S. suits, the technicians had their throats crushed by metal gloves. The C.A.D.S. suits had been called to action, called by their human leader, and these men had gotten in their way. They killed without malice. And the C.A.D.S. suits continued to use their systems to scan the fort and locate the source of the words that had called them to life. Zeus's artificial-intelligence circuits made decision after decision based upon its analysis of what its owner would do. It had studied Sturgis over the past weeks, studied and learned. And if a metal thing with a brain of synthetic chips and memory boards could like someone, it liked its owner! It wanted to rescue Sturgis!

Back in the colonel's cell, it was rat feeding time again. The rat-tube door opened time after time, and each time it let in a dozen starved rats. Sturgis took on the first waves of hungry rodents gamely, but when the torture was repeated, when the ante went up to eighteen rats at a time, the colonel was fading away. This was too hard to do. Naked, he couldn't keep up the fight.

He was exhausted within five minutes of his "prayer" session, and when the next wave of rats came at him, he received several serious bites. The minutes dragged on like hours. He stomped them, smashed them with his bloodied fists, and he even bit one to death, but Sturgis knew it was only a matter of time until he would be all through. He just couldn't take another such attack. As he stomped out the last frenzied opponent, the colonel sank to the floor, breathing in huge gulps of foul air.

"Send in another three dozen rats," Veloshnikov hissed out over the speaker.

Sturgis groaned in the agony that only lost souls feel.

Chapter Twenty-eight

The C.A.D.S. commander heard the sound of screams, shots, and then metal bending. The cellblock's main door broke open and in stepped a C.A.D.S. suit. A suit with no face inside its clear visor! His prayers had been answered. As the new rat-arrivals poured into his cell, the exhausted nuke-trooper called out, "Zeus, I'm over here! Get me out of this cell."

The automaton-suit strode over to the cell and a metal glove-hand reached out and tore the cell doors loose. "Zeus!" Sturgis ordered, "Uncouple yourself to prepare for human entry." The suit dutifully fired its de-connect bolts and collapsed into pieces.

The colonel quickly slipped into the C.A.D.S. armor outfit and sealed up, then purposefully strode toward the exit, as frenzied rats bit at his metallic body. He needed some ammo right now. And he found it. The dead guards, lying with their necks snapped outside the cell-blocks, had several automatic weapons. The colonel quickly emptied their weapons' magazines into the VSF unit on his right sleeve. The suit readout came on: "MANUAL FIRING SYSTEM LOADED. THREE HUNDRED TWELVE 9 MM SHELLS."

He smiled. The VSF was fast and reliable. It had automatically assimilated the bullets and readied them for firing.

Sirens were going off all over the place. Sturgis saw cans of kerosene piled up in the corridor and got an idea. Kerosene wasn't exactly the compound of napalm and gasoline that the C.A.D.S. unit's flamethrower was used to, but it would do! He poured several cans of the liquid into his tank and then he was off down the corridor, walking right into the hail of bullets fired by a group of Anetra's Pods.

The colonel yelled, "Flame mode. Activate!" He pointed his right arm's weapon-tube and like a Greek god of old he threw fire at the opposition. The kerosene didn't burn quite as well as napalm, but it did the job. Screaming and aflame, the soldiers of Anetra ceased to be a problem.

"Ouch! What the hell," Sturgis shouted as he felt a sharp sting in his left ankle. Damn it! There was obviously a rat in his suit, biting his leg. Sturgis considered de-suiting until another phalanx of human opponents arrayed themselves against him and started firing. He had to keep the suit on. So he tried another strategy. He slammed his leg down again and again with full servo-assisted force, jarring the hell out of himself and shaking the rat down under his bare foot. And then the next time he jumped, his heel snapped the ribcage of the rat and it stopped being a problem. And started being a sticky mess.

Sturgis then squished down the hall, firing his stolen bullets accurately to cut down the group of mercenaries standing in his way. He had to find the other men of his unit. Had they too been rescued, or was he the only lucky one?

But his thought was answered as the suit's radio crackled into life with Billy Dixon's voice. "Skip," the southerner yelled out, "Damnedest thing! My empty suit busted into my cell and rescued me. Now I'm up on G level, where the hell are you?"

"Heading your way Billy, heading your way," the colonel exclaimed as he rushed into a stairwell and began climbing at thirty miles per hour. "If you find Jeeters, tell him to cancel the destruction. We can defeat this whole bunch of assholes in our C.A.D.S. armor, I think." When he got to G level—evidently where the other C.A.D.S. men had been incarcerated—Sturgis was greeted with an unusual sight: Several other C.A.D.S. suits were walking around out in the corridor, some banging up against the bulkhead-like walls of the fort, others spinning on their own feet. They hadn't quite got the hang of automatic pilot, he guessed.

Then an occupied suit came running up. The I.D. Mode said it was Billy, and the colonel soon saw the platinum blond youth's smiling face inside the visor of the unit. "Skip," Billy said, "it's a fucking miracle. Fenton, Tranh and Fireheels are free too, and they're in their suits. We've been stealing ammo everywhere! They're down the hall loading up their systems from a mini-ammo depot."

"Lead on," the colonel said, "I could use a fix of some good old heavy shells."

When the colonel and Billy reached the ammo, he found that Martel and one of the troopers they'd recruited at White Sands, Jones, were on the scene too. They were there loading up ammo by the carload.

"Okay, enough," the colonel ordered. "We have to find the others—and the President. And Jeeters. Above all find the reverend. We have to stop him from blowing up the fort. Let's go."

Then the sirens wailing all around them were overridden by a more ominous beeping note. The horrible words spoken by a computer's female voice echoed through the fort: "MAIN NUCLEAR PILE GOING CRITICAL. MELTDOWN IN TEN MINUTES."

"Men," Sturgis said in a voice more like a curse, "Jeeters has done his job only too well! We have ten minutes to find our friends and get them — and ourselves — several miles from here! Now *go*. Spread out, and we meet at the main entrance door we came down from. In eight minutes. No more. Round up all our friends that you can."

His thoughts right now were on two things above all: Finding Morgana and the loss of Robin. Robin, he had to realize, no matter how alive she looked, was gone. The colonel had to face that. He thought to take her body with him, give her a proper burial. No. He knew one thing about cryogenic freezing: You can't just pull something out of a tank like that! She'd shatter into a million pieces. Robin's body would be nuked along with all the others in the fort, within — nine minutes! No time for tears, there were people to rescue. The tears would flow later.

Sturgis, keeping in touch with the other active C.A.D.S. troopers by radio and scan-systems, went up two levels to the main esplanade as the others spread out in their searches. He struggled past masses of entangled cultists and Pinky-mercenaries. They were no bother to him because they were all at each other's throats, swinging knives, shooting one another. It was a friggin' civil war, while the seconds ticked off toward a Gotterdammerung!

That civil war, the colonel realized, made it easier for his side. Maybe they *could* find the President and the others, and get out of the fort. "Morgana," he mumbled to himself, "Got to find Morgana." He was damned glad now that before they left White Sands, all personnel — including Morgana — had been "tagged" with a signalling computer-chip injected into their arm. Including the frail beauty he now sought to find.

The computer-chip didn't have much range, however, and it was a long while running around before Sturgis's search through the madness of the fort was rewarded. "MORGANA PINTER LOCATED," his readout stated. And it gave him the bearings. Sturgis ran as fast as his metalman muscles could allow, tearing through some walls, throwing an occasional cultist or mercenary aside as he headed to the rescue of Morgana.

He found her chained to a wall in a cell in Area A. She had been tortured. Welts from whips, and small burn marks from hot instruments scarred several tender areas of her pale nude body. She was barely conscious.

Sturgis smiled as the scar-faced Soviet officer that had been tormenting her turned in horror when the colonel came into view. He was still holding a cigarette in his hand. A cigarette that had produced one of Morgana's many burns.

"School's out," Sturgis intoned, and sent out a hail of smg fire that cut the pervert down. More than that — the bullets ripped him in half.

As the officer fell wide-eyed, staring at not the ceiling but the hell that he was entering, Sturgis cut Morgana down. He took a uniform jacket hanging on a hook and slipped her arms into the large sleeves. Then he carried her off toward the surface.

"FOUR MINUTES TO DETONATION," the cold voice of the computer intoned as he rushed up the last fifty stairs.

Tranh met Sturgis. The Vietnamese-American trooper was stabilizing a sag-kneed President Williamson with metal arms. Fenton and Billy were there too, each with their small group of rescued Americans.

"Come on, Skip," Fenton said, "This is it! Let's get out of here."

"No," Sturgis ordered, "Not me. Here, take Morgana," he said, handing her over to Billy. "You men all head to the surface. Get a mile away and shield the civilians with your bodies, if you can't find rock-shelter. I'm going back down to C level. I think I can find Jeeters. *You go! Now!*"

"Yessir," they all replied. It was hard for them to obey, for they were all hero-types. But each of the men knew better than to argue when time was too short. Someone had to get the handful of rescued personnel to safety.

Chapter Twenty-nine

The instant that the nuclear pile of the fort began to go critical, Veloshnikov had gone into action. The Russian leader wondered for just a fraction of a second how the hell Sturgis had pulled *this* coup, then he concentrated on the task at hand: Survival.

Ignoring the royal couple's plea for his advice on what to do, the supreme marshal rushed from their throne room and joined up with his own men. He bemoaned the imminent loss of the greatest military facility on earth while they rushed upward, using the staircase for fear that the elevators would lose power. He cursed the fact that the throne room was in the deepest part of the fort. He knew that he must climb thirty-seven stories in order to reach the surface. In order to begin the run for life. In order to get miles away before the explosion. Huffing and puffing, he wasn't sure he was up to the climb.

Worse, as the Soviet officer reached the upper floors, he encountered many others just as desperate for survival. Crowds of mercenaries and cultists literally climbed over and trampled one another, clogging the stairs. And the acrid fumes of fires, the staccato reports of gunfire, the screams made it all a living hell. Soon Veloshnikov and his men were down to climbing over fallen bodies, living and dead. And then he was immobilized in the seething madness. And Veloshnikov realized that he *wasn't going to make it.*

"No! I won't die!" Veloshnikov shouted, and he directed orders at his men: "Back down, go back down!" Slowly his men extricated themselves and they helped him to his feet. They started back down the stairs. There were suddenly no lights except for their emergency flashbeams. "The power is off! The elevators are stopped," one of his men shouted. "I can hear those trapped in the elevators screaming."

The Russian leader said, "There must be another way up! Maybe . . . maybe we can find one of those Sky-tanks and *blast* our way up to the surface. That's it! Head toward the garage-section! There must be a vehicle ramp to the surface! It is my duty to the Soviet Union to survive."

His eyes were blurred and tearing now — not only from the smoke and fumes on the stairs, but from the horrid realization that he might not live to enjoy world domination.

Meanwhile, Pinky and Anetra had left their throne room. They had tried to follow their Russian guest toward safety, but an explosion had ripped apart the corridor before them, and sealed them in. And that was that.

They were now back in their master bedroom, where the fires had not yet reached. They had stripped to their underwear, pulling the last of each other's garments open with violent tugs. It didn't take a nuclear scientist to realize what was happening. If they were to die, each had decided, they wanted to die making love.

They flopped on the giant bed and got right to it. Anetra, between passionate kisses, told Pinky, "This is just like in my dreams. I predicted this long ago! I know that this is the end of the world, as predicted in the sacred Mayan texts. In my divine visions I saw this! I saw the destruction, the fire, the blood. I knew it was coming. I just didn't expect it to be today!"

"Hold me Anetra. Make love to me." They rolled on the bed, naked, clumsy in their desperation.

Pinky wasn't up to the task. He was suddenly not at all so sure that rolling in the hay was what they should be doing. There *must* be some way to survive, he thought.

But Anetra was all over him and she had him pinned to the sheets with her huge mass. "This is just like Hitler and Eva Brawn in the bunker in Berlin," she cooed. "They died together, like gods entering the eternal flame. We will die like they did!"

Conflicting emotions raged through the naked emperor. And slowly but surely, a force, a desire more powerfully ingrained in Pinky than even sex was winning that raging battle for control.

Fear.

Pinky whined, "No! I'm not gonna die! That story about Hitler and his dame is romantic bunk. A fabrication. I read all about how they burned some other couple — the Nussbaums — in the bunker. And then they both took a plane to Rio."

"That's not true," Anetra complained, "don't you insult Adolph and Eva! Now, get going! We only have a few minutes to make love. Come on honey, do it to me good! Let us be joined together when the end comes! Don't be frightened, my love. We are together. There is no fear when there is ultimate love. Make love to me. But hold off climaxing. Let's not have one of your quickies. There are two minutes till detonation. Come inside me just when the reactor goes off. We'll have a nuclear-climax, and meet again in the next world to love again."

"I don't *believe* that we will really live again, Anetra," Pinky shouted, totally giving up trying to get his spongy

207

manhood between the huge thighs.

"Aren't you a romantic, Pinky? Don't you believe in reincarnation? It's a fact, you know. I remember my last life as the Goddess of Atlantis. Surely you don't doubt my word. Now, put your goddamned pecker inside me and get cracking!"

Pinky just couldn't resign himself to dying. He tore loose from her sweaty body and stood up and screamed, "You broads! You're all the same." He went to the dresser and opened the top drawer and took out a German Luger. "You die, bitch, I'm getting out of here," he snarled. And then Pinky levelled the gun on the naked mass of female pulcritude. And he fired.

It took several shots to finish her off, but finally Anetra's eyes, tearful with disappointment more than pain, rolled up. Her lips spouted blood like a fountain as she said her last words: "You're a prick."

The gurgling blood made it sound to Pinky more like she said, "You're a blick."

He was grateful that she hadn't fallen in front of the door. "Anetra," he said, as a final retort, "I loved you. But I don't die for no broad!" Then he dashed out into the corridor filled with smoke. Two of his mercenaries were down on the carpet, using crowbars to pry open a duct screen. Pinky realized that they had found a way out. Just as they popped open the screen, he shot them with his last two bullets and then he crawled inside the duct.

Luckily, it was a big air-conduit, and wide enough for his passage. He crawled for all he was worth, choking on smoke, until he reached fresher air. And Pinky saw that he was inside a wall overlooking the motor-pool of the fort.

"DETONATION IN ONE MINUTE," the computer announced without emotion.

Chapter Thirty

While Pinky — and separately, Veloshnikov — made their desperate bids for survival, Sturgis was heading in the opposite direction: He was going back down into the bowels of the fort to find Jeeters. He hadn't time to explain to his men why he thought he could find Jeeters. Besides, he could be wrong. But he had tried to think like Jeeters, to get some idea as to where the reverend might go if he knew that the fort was going to explode.

In order to start the destruct sequence, the colonel knew, Jeeters would have gone via tunnel 333 to the reactor. Yes — and then what? Most men, knowing that they couldn't possibly make it to safety in so short a time, would have just sat down and had a smoke right there, in the reactor-room, to wait for the end. But Sturgis felt that Jeeters wouldn't do that. Sturgis had an inkling that Reverend Jeeters would go to church. A reverend surely would wish to pray his way into the next world!

So the colonel had rapidly consulted the computer-stored partial grid map of the fort, and found an area marked chapel. "Direct me to the chapel," he had ordered and the suit's computer complied.

Now, as he reached level B, his holographic visor-screen was suddenly filled with lines and arrows superimposed on his view of the stairs ahead. He followed the helpful computer's directions toward the chapel. Luckily, the chapel was only five flights down from where he had left the C.A.D.S. men and the rescued civvies, just a quarter mile north.

With the servo-drive power-assist giving his stride the power of a Mack truck in overdrive, the colonel's cleated boots made dents in the steel decking as he ran. A ten minute run by an athlete was accomplished in twenty seconds.

He smiled as he saw the sign over an ornate wooden door emblazoned with painted figures of saints. The chapel. But just as he was ready to cross the last twenty feet of corridor and open the chapel's double doors, a problem developed. A formidable set of opponents, much more dangerous than the cultists and khaki-clad mercenaries he had exterminated earlier, blocked his way.

They were shouting in Russian. Six black-clad Soviet commandos. And they were targeting him with their sten-guns before he could even think of moving, catching Sturgis in a withering crossfire. Only his armor kept him from being chewed into little pieces of raw meat. And he dove to the floor as one of the Reds unleashed a bazooka shell at him that would have torn even the C.A.D.S. suit apart.

Sturgis rolled awkwardly on the flooring and responded with LPF mode; the quickest way to eliminate six guys in one sweep. The super heated kerosene flames shot out of his firing tube and the Sovs burst into balls of flames. They became screaming torches. They fired a few more rounds of smg fire as they fell. Sturgis just let the bullets ping off his suit as he regained his footing and opened the chapel door. He faced a candlelit row of seats that had a plain golden cross glinting at their far end.

"Jeeters, you in here? It's Sturgis. I can get you out!" He thought he saw a moving dark shape toward the far side of

210

the chapel, but couldn't make it out. It was too dark to really see, so Sturgis commanded, "Infra-red screen! Night vision!"

And he suddenly could see clearly. The dark shape was a man, who had been bent on his knees before the cross in prayer.

"Colonel! How did you—"

"Never mind, Jeeters," Sturgis said, scooping the reverend up in his metal arms and kicking open the doors which had swung shut. He rushed toward the stairs that led to the surface.

"DETONATION IN THREE MINUTES," the computer intoned.

He reached the stairs and found that he wasn't the only one attempting to use it. A mass of frenzied cultists were scrambling up the concrete steps, climbing over one another. Sturgis held Jeeters up over his head and trampled up through them, breaking legs and arms and tumbling cultists under his feet until he was once again on the upper level.

He faced ten more Sov commandos. What the hell was with these guys? Why did they bother to shoot at people? You'd think they'd either be trying to escape themselves, or just sitting out the end with a vodka bottle jammed down their throats!

They fired some sort of gas shells in his direction, almost before the colonel could set Jeeters down and use his own weapons. The colonel's armor took the slugs and then he moved them down with a sweep of his firing tube set for maximum fire of the explosive bullets he carried. There was little left of the Sov to fall down and lie quivering on the floor. The Sov commandos were reduced to just pulp and blood splashed on the far wall.

Jeeters started choking when one of the gas-shells the Sovs had fired popped. Instantly, the reverend turned blue. Sturgis, cursing like mad, grabbed him up and again took off toward the exit ramp. He hoped to hell the reverend wouldn't die after all that he'd gone through to rescue him!

When Sturgis reached the area that he had last encountered his men, they were gone, as he had ordered. He immediately headed for the blinding light of the desert that was visible through half open blast-doors to the right. He could see some rocky hills about a mile away — maybe he could make it. Maybe the fresh wind would revive Jeeters.

"TWO MINUTES TO DETONATION," the computer voice said.

Sturgis didn't waste a second. He just tore-ass toward those hills. Soon he was hitting fifty miles per hour on his super-drive legs. A nuke-age Jesse Owens trying for the gold medal called survival!

Was his speed good enough? The computer in his suit told him the sad tale: "PROBABILITY OF DESTRUCTION OF THIS UNIT IS 100%, UNDER CURRENT CIRCUMSTANCES."

He kept running, anyway. But now was as good a time as any to seek the advice of the Zeus-artificial intelligence system in the suit. "Zeus," Sturgis asked, between huffing breaths, "Any way to survive?"

"SUGGEST TAKING COURSE 33 DEGREES TO NORTH. SEVERAL PARKED AIR-VEHICLES LOCATED THERE."

"Will do!" the colonel shouted. Boy, this new Zeus system was something *else!* He had never gotten suggestions from his suit before! He veered in the direction indicated and headed for the parked Soviet jets he now scanned ahead. As he approached, the Lifeprobe-mode showed no signs of humans around. The pilots and guards must have headed for the fort when they heard the sirens, to see what the hell was going on. Now if someone only left the ignition key to one of these sleek babies . . .

Sturgis climbed up on the wing of one of the closest jets and peered into the open canopy. No key. He tried the second jet, a bigger job. Yes! There *was* a key dangling in a slot next to the attenuated steering wheel that steered it. He plopped Jeeters's unconscious form in the seat behind the pilot seat and pushed the seat all the way back and squeezed into it without removing his C.A.D.S. armor. He studied the dials and buttons for a moment and then shrugged. "Computer," he queried, "any suggestions on how to fly this thing?"

"Affirmative," the suit's computer responded. The A.I. chips were sure doing double duty today!

Following the computer directions, Sturgis got the ramjet engines flaming out power and began hurtling down the packed sand of the prairie in the opposite direction from the fort, crushed back in his seat by massive acceleration.

Without a second thought about the fact he hadn't flown a jet like this one ever, the colonel took off when the speedometer needle crossed the red line. He broke the sound barrier just as he left the ground and shot over the low hills and brought the delta-wing craft down to twenty feet over the ground once more, tearing up cacti with the shock wave of his passage.

And then he saw the flash. Or rather saw the reflection of the nuclear explosion behind him in the sky ahead. The shock wave rocked his jet a second later, but by that time, the colonel and Jeeters were fifty miles away from ground zero.

Chapter Thirty-one

"Over here," Billy yelled, "the best shelter is over here."

The eleven surviving C.A.D.S. men, each carrying one or two of the civilian escapees from Fort Collins, followed the southern nuke-trooper's directions. They rushed into the rock shelter after him. They huddled down, placing the civilians in the deepest part of the twenty-foot-deep natural enclosure. Then the C.A.D.S. men used their metal-clad bodies to cover the others from danger.

Billy heaved a sigh of relief. They were about a mile and a half from Fort Collins, and the shelter was solid granite and faced away from the fort. They might survive the coming explosion.

"Sixteen seconds to detonation," Tranh announced. "FIFTEEN-FOURTEEN . . ." There was a terrible thunderclap and then a wwwhhhooooossssshhhh! overhead.

"What the hell was that, Billy?" Fenton asked. "Was that the explosion? That wasn't so bad."

"It was a jet," Billy said, "and I sure as hell hope that the colonel was aboard it, because . . ."

"THREE, TWO, ONE, ZER—"

The whole sky lit up, and then the granite shook like it was a bowl of gray jello. Small rocks fell among the troopers and their charges, and clouds of dust loosened by the titanic shock wave flew about. The rescued civilians were soon coughing and choking, but Billy didn't let anyone get up and go out until the second shock wave rolled by. No way was he going to lose any of the people he and his fellow troopers had worked so desperately to save.

Within a minute after the blast, they crawled out into the reddish-lit desert once more. And Billy turned and beheld the roiling hundred-thousand-foot-high mushroom shaped cloud. That was the end of Fort Collins and a hell of a lot of good guys and bad guys too.

Tranh shouted, "My long-distance radar has picked up the jet again. It's turning in our direction and coming in low. Get everyone down."

But before anyone could move, the dart-like Soviet craft already shot past overhead, and it rocked on its wings. A victory salute.

Over the C.A.D.S. channel came a familiar voice, "Colonel Sturgis and Jerry Jeff Jeeters say hello!" Then the crackling signal in their communicators was lost in a storm of nuclear generated static.

A small group of the survivors climbed up a smooth dome of rock to get a better view of the sky to the east, where the jet had gone. President Williamson was among them. He came over to stand between Tranh and Billy, the gray-haired Williamson looking frail and insignificant next to the seven-foot-tall metal armored warriors. Williamson stared up at the smoke-trail left by the jet. "Was that —"

"Yes," Tranh reported on audi-mode, "The colonel and Reverend Jeeters are alive, in that jet. I expect the colonel will come around and land in a minute or so."

Fenton carried Morgana, whose oversized coveralls were all covered with dust, over to the small group that was staring up at the sky. She had heard the news and was smiling despite her pains. All of them had lost dear friends, and some of the civilians had lost their children

215

down there. But there was no wailing, no moaning in the group. Instead, they just stood there in the warm breeze, silhouetted in the dull-red false dawn that the nuke-explosion had left smearing the sky. Billy was keeping track of the radiation level. It was okay for now, as the nuke cloud was blowing away toward the north. But soon, he knew, they would have to move on.

"She's coming around," Fenton said. "My bet is the Skip will set that jet down as close to us as he can."

Indeed, the Soviet jet was expertly guided in by their commander, and soon its tires squealed upon contact with the desert floor just a hundred yards beyond where they stood.

"That jet Skip is flying is a transport job," Tranh noted with some cheer. "We probably can all cram into it."

"Terrific. Then, if it has fuel enough, we can go —" Billy just stopped talking. White Sands Base was gone, and now Fort Collins was just a melt hole in the desert. Where the hell could they go?

Later, the mute survivors all sat around a campfire. Fenton MacLeish had managed to make coffee and they all had a go at some canned rations they found in the big Soviet jet.

Everyone was waiting for Sturgis or the President to decide what to do. They had been conferring for about a half hour, ever since shortly after the colonel had landed.

Williamson, ironically in much better health because of the medical treatment he had received in the fort, suggested to the colonel that they fly toward the east. He thought they could find one of the freedom fighter bases along the Mississippi. If there was enough fuel for the flight there.

Sturgis shook his head in disagreement. He pointed out, "We haven't managed to save young Chris, nor a

216

single one of the eastern freedom fighters. And Jeeters doesn't know the location of any of those exact bases. The Reds controlled much of the land east of the Mississippi River. I suggest that we fly the short distance back to the Naqui Indian reservation. Chief Naktu is among our survivors. He says we would be welcome back in his camp. There are supplies — even fuel — back there," Sturgis concluded. "All we have are the shirts on our backs and the C.A.D.S. suits."

Williamson spilled out his cold coffee. He didn't like the idea of going to the Indian reservation one bit. But with a little more discussion, he finally agreed that the colonel's proposal was the safest alternative.

Sturgis stood up, silhouetted by the campfire and announced the decision. "We will fly to the Naqui lands. — Any comments?"

"Colonel," the southerner asked, "Are we sure that we're the only survivors?"

Sturgis looked hard at Billy and said, "Well, we scanned the area for fifty miles in all directions for signs of life, and found not a living thing besides some singed coyotes and rabbits. I'd say that we're probably the only ones to make it out. Anyone who couldn't run as fast as you men did in C.A.D.S. suits — or get a jet up in the air — didn't make it. They're all gone. There's just some atoms left of all our dear friends and hated enemies." He looked down at the ground and his voice trailed off as a tear formed in his right eye. Robin was gone too.

The President, clad in a Soviet Air Force sweater and a pair of khaki pants, was sipping another, warmer cup of coffee like it was Chock-Full-O'Nuts best. He stopped long enough to say, "Dean is right. Wishing it weren't so doesn't make it so. We have wounded among us that need treatment, so we can't just stay here forever and look for stragglers. Joe Fireheels has some burns. And Jones has a damned bullet lodged in his shoulder. And three of the civilians are as bad off—Carter, Mrs. McGinty and Jason Hodges. We will find help at the reservation."

Rossiter stood up. "Mr. President?"

"Yes, Mickey."

"What's to happen to the U.S. now? I mean without the base, with just the few of us left."

"I don't know," the President said, looking up at the distended black clouds low on the horizon to the north — the leftover of the nuke explosion. "But at least the Reds don't have the fort. At least Pinky is dead, and Anetra and her cultists. And Marshal Veloshnikov too. That alone should put a grinding halt to the Soviet aims of world empire. One thing I do know. We tend to think of ourselves as the *whole* United States. But we know there are millions of loyal Americans out there, all over the place. Other Americans fighting the Soviet invaders everywhere, fighting with whatever they can get their hands on! America will go on, until it is triumphant. It's not having a particular fort or base that will make us win. It's *moxie*."

"Yeah," Sturgis added. "And I expect the Reds will be busy fighting among themselves for a while. We can regroup. There will be a new battle for power in the Kremlin, once they know that their head-honcho Veloshnikov bit the dust."

The President had the last word before they all filed aboard the Sov transport jet: "We should consider what happened today a victory, and we should remember that our friends did not die in vain. The greatest threat to America's survival has been eliminated. We can do without the fort, we did without it before! We're going to find a new home for the White House, set up a new government—by election, as always. And as long as the thought of freedom exists, America exists."

Epilogue

Sturgis was wrong about his group being the only survivors. There were at least two other survivors of the Fort Collins explosion.

Sixty-one miles to the southwest, a lone battered armor-vehicle bounced along the rolling desert, moving on four blown tires. The driver was a man whose face — already full of scars from years ago — had some fresh, raw new wounds. He had all his front teeth missing and his left eye socket was missing the eyeball that used to be there. Oozing blood and pus leaked down from that wound. The man could hardly breathe. His ribs were cracked and every breath was an agony. But he lived.

He was Supreme Marshal Veloshnikov, would-be ruler of the world. And he had managed to escape a mile from the fort in this heavily armored behemoth before the nuke exploded. The fifty-ton heavy-armor vehicle had been thrown up into the air like a Tonka-toy model by the explosion. He had been battered as it finally landed again and rolled over and over, caught in the shock wave.

But he lived. And he would live, he told himself, long enough to wreak revenge on the man who had done this! Somehow Sturgis had blown up the fort, there was no doubt in his mind.

The second survivor unknown to the colonel's party was unconscious. She slept, breathing heavy foul air, inside a spherical eight-foot-wide metal capsule immersed in deep cool water. The scorched metal ball had once been covered with frost, but now it glowed red hot on the outside. Inside, it was one hundred ten degrees Farenheit, and that temperature was, despite the chilly water, still climbing.

The capsule was the only thing left of the entire underground fort it had rested in. It existed because it had started out super-cold to begin with. And because it had been blown by the blast into a natural underground chamber filled with water. The spherical S.A. chamber had smashed itself into the water filled cavern like a meteor, hit the waters of the nether-world river, and splashed deep down.

Now it slowly rose back up, heading toward the earth's surface. The capsule floated along in the water that began rising into the mild wide crater that the nuclear explosion had created.

The person inside the spherical metal capsule was Robin Adler. And she just slept, she was not dead. Her body temperature was one hundred five degrees Farenheit. It had been raised from minus four hundred degrees in just a fraction of a second, when Fort Collins had been vaporized by the nuclear blast. That sudden unfreezing approximated the process necessary to restore life to someone who was quick-frozen. But she would soon die if the air was not replenished, if the temperature of the capsule didn't lower.

The metal ball reached the surface of the vast crater in the titanic geyser of underground trapped water. The force of the water made it fly up into the air a thousand feet. Then it fell back, and splashed back. Bobbing along, it cascaded toward the west, spinning round and round near the edge of the rushing water.

The capsule with the limp female form inside it brushed past the boulders of the inundated desert and moved on.

An hour later, it was miles away from the place it originated, and it came into sight of a lone prospector named Murchison. The old man riding a spotted-mule named Amy had to retreat up a steep hill to avoid the flash flood.

The prospector cursed and cursed the waters blocking his way until he saw the capsule floating by. And then he followed along the raging new river, intrigued. He followed until the receding flood left the capsule high and dry on a sandbar.

The old codger dismounted Amy and waddled over to the strange thing. Maybe, he thought, it could be valuable. Maybe it had something in it he could use.

And when he scrambled down to have a peek at the strange thing, he saw the small window. Peering inside it, he saw a woman inside the scorched and smoky magna-glass.

Murchison, being a Bible-reading man, immediately thought of Moses, who had sailed down the Nile in a basket. She was like Moses, only more beautiful, of course. He fumbled with the lock-device on the door of the capsule. It felt hot, but tolerably so. And he managed to spring some hidden mechanism. The door hissed open with a foul rush of air. And the woman inside suddenly opened her eyes. She seemed not to see him for a moment, then her brown eyes focused on his face.

"You all right in there, miss?" he asked.

"I don't know," Robin replied. "I — I guess so,"

"Say, miss, would you like some help to get out of there?"

"I — I suppose so."

He helped her get out, and then the prospector asked, "What's your name?"

Robin looked blank. And she finally said, "I really don't know."